The

SCHOOL

of

ESSENTIAL

INGREDIENTS

The
SCHOOL
of
ESSENTIAL
INGREDIENTS

Erica Bauermeister

G. P. PUTNAM'S SONS
New York

PUTNAM

G. P. PUTNAM'S SONS
Publishers Since 1838
Published by the Penguin Group
Penguin Group (USA) Inc., 375 Hudson Street, New York, New York 10014,
USA • Penguin Group (Canada), 90 Eglinton Avenue East, Suite 700, Toronto, Ontario
M4P 2Y3, Canada (a division of Pearson Canada Inc.) • Penguin Books Ltd, 80 Strand,
London WC2R 0RL, England • Penguin Ireland, 25 St Stephen's Green, Dublin 2,
Ireland (a division of Penguin Books Ltd) • Penguin Group (Australia),
250 Camberwell Road, Camberwell, Victoria 3124, Australia (a division of Pearson Australia
Group Pty Ltd) • Penguin Books India Pvt Ltd, 11 Community Centre, Panchsheel Park,
New Delhi–110 017, India • Penguin Group (NZ), 67 Apollo Drive, Rosedale,
North Shore 0632, New Zealand (a division of Pearson New Zealand Ltd) • Penguin Books
(South Africa) (Pty) Ltd, 24 Sturdee Avenue, Rosebank, Johannesburg 2196, South Africa

Penguin Books Ltd, Registered Offices:
80 Strand, London WC2R 0RL, England

Library of Congress Cataloging-in-Publication Data

Bauermeister, Erica.
The school of essential ingredients / Erica Bauermeister.
p.   cm.
ISBN 978-0-399-15543-7
1. Women cooks—Fiction.   2. Cooking schools—Fiction.
3. Friendship—Fiction.   I. Title.
PS3602.A9357S36   2009   2008029728
813'.6—dc22

Printed in the United States of America
1   3   5   7   9   10   8   6   4   2

BOOK DESIGN BY AMANDA DEWEY
ILLUSTRATIONS BY GLORIA ATTOUN

For Heidi, Karin, and Dad

The

SCHOOL

of

ESSENTIAL

INGREDIENTS

Prologue

L illian loved best the moment before she turned on the lights. She would stand in the restaurant kitchen doorway, rain-soaked air behind her, and let the smells come to her—ripe sourdough yeast, sweet-dirt coffee, and garlic, mellowing as it lingered. Under them, more elusive, stirred the faint essence of fresh meat, raw tomatoes, cantaloupe, water on lettuce. Lillian breathed in, feeling the smells move about and through her, even as she searched out those that might suggest a rotting orange at the bottom of a pile, or whether the new assistant chef was still double-dosing the curry dishes. She was. The girl was a daughter of a friend and good enough with knives, but some days, Lillian thought with a sigh, it was like trying to teach subtlety to a thunderstorm.

But tonight was Monday. No assistant chefs, no customers

looking for solace or celebration. Tonight was Monday, cooking-class night.

After seven years of teaching, Lillian knew how her students would arrive on the first night of class—walking through the kitchen door alone or in ad hoc groups of two or three that had met up on the walkway to the mostly darkened restaurant, holding the low, nervous conversations of strangers who will soon touch one another's food. Once inside, some would clump together, making those first motions toward connection, while others would roam the kitchen, fingers stroking brass pots or picking up a glowing red pepper, like small children drawn to the low-hanging ornaments on a Christmas tree.

Lillian loved to watch her students at this moment—they were elements that would become more complex and intriguing as they mixed with one another, but at the beginning, placed in relief by their unfamiliar surroundings, their essence was clear. A young man reaching out to touch the shoulder of the still younger woman next to him—"What's your name?"—as her hand dropped to the stainless-steel counter and traced its smooth surface. Another woman standing alone, her mind still lingering with—a child? a lover? Every once in a while there was a couple, in love or ruins.

Lillian's students arrived with a variety of motivations, some drawn by a yearning as yet unmet to hear murmured culinary compliments, others who had come to find a cook rather than become one. A few participants had no desire for lessons at all, arriving with gift certificates in hand as if on a forced march to certain failure; they knew their cakes would always be flat, their cream sauces filled with small, disconcerting pockets of flour, like bills in your mailbox when you had hoped for a love letter.

And then there were those students who seemingly had no choice, who could no more stay out of a kitchen than a kleptomaniac could keep her hands in her pockets. They came early, stayed late, fantasized about leaving their corporate jobs and becoming chefs with an exhilarating mixture of guilt and pleasure. If Lillian's soul sought out this last group, it was only to be expected, but in truth, she found them all fascinating. Lillian knew that whatever their reasons for coming, at some moment in the course of the class each one's eyes would widen with joy or tears or resolution—it always happened. The timing and the reason would be different for each, and that's where the fascination lay. No two spices work the same.

The kitchen was ready. The long stainless-steel counters lay before her, expansive and cool in the dark. Lillian knew without looking that Robert had received the vegetable order from the produce man who delivered only on Mondays. Caroline would have stood over skinny, smart-mouthed Daniel until the floors were scrubbed, the thick rubber mats rinsed with the hose outside until they were black and shining. Beyond the swinging door on the other side of the kitchen, the dining room stood ready, a quiet field of tables under starched white linen, napkins folded into sharp triangles at each place. But no one would use the dining room tonight. All that mattered was the kitchen.

Lillian stretched her fingers once, twice, and turned on the light.

Lillian

L illian had been four years old when her father left them, and her mother, stunned, had slid into books like a seal into water. Lillian had watched her mother submerge and disappear, sensing instinctively even at her young age the impersonal nature of a choice made simply for survival, and adapting to the niche she would now inhabit, as a watcher from the shore of her mother's ocean.

In this new life, Lillian's mother's face became a series of book covers, held in place where eyes, nose, or mouth might normally appear. Lillian soon learned that book covers could forecast moods much like facial expressions, for Lillian's mother swam deeply into the books she read, until the personality of the protagonist surrounded her like a perfume applied by an indiscriminate hand. Lillian was never sure who would greet her at the breakfast table, no matter that the bathrobe, the hair, the feet were always the same. It was like having a magician for a mother, although Lillian always suspected that the magicians she saw at birthday parties went home and turned back into portly men with three children and grass that needed mowing. Lillian's mother simply finished one book and turned to the next.

Her mother's preoccupation with books was not an entirely silent occupation. Long before Lillian's father had left them, long before Lillian knew that words had a meaning beyond the music of their inflections, her mother had read aloud to her. Not from cardboard books with their primary-colored illustrations and monosyllabic rhymes. Lillian's mother dismissed the few that entered their house under the guise of guilt.

"There's no need to eat potatoes, Lily," she would say, "when four-course meals are ready and waiting." And she would read.

For Lillian's mother, every part of a book was magic, but what she delighted in most were the words themselves. Lillian's mother collected exquisite phrases and complicated rhythms, descriptions that undulated across a page like cake batter pour-ing into a pan, read aloud to put the words in the air, where she could hear as well as see them.

"Oh, Lily," her mother would say, "listen to this one. It sounds green, don't you think?"

And Lillian, who was too young to know that words were not colors and thoughts were not sounds, would listen while the syllables fell quietly through her, and she would think, *This is what green sounds like.*

After Lillian's father left, however, things changed, and she increasingly came to see herself simply as a mute and obliging assistant in the accumulation of exceptional phrases, or, if they happened to be somewhere public, as her mother's social cover. People would smile at the vision of a mother nurturing her daughter's literary imagination, but Lillian knew better. In Lillian's mind, her mother was a museum for words; Lillian was an annex, necessary when space became limited in the original building.

Not surprisingly, when it came time for Lillian to learn to read, she balked. It was not only an act of defiance, although by the time kindergarten started, Lillian was already feeling toward books private surges of aggression that left her both confused and slightly powerful. But it wasn't just that. In Lillian's world, books were covers and words were sound and movement, not form. She could not equate the rhythms that had insinuated themselves into her imagination with what she saw on the paper. The letters lay prone across the page, arranged in unyielding precision. There was no magic on the page itself, Lillian saw; and while this increased Lillian's estimation of her mother's abilities, it did nothing to further her interest in books.

IT WAS DURING Lillian's first skirmishes with the printed word that she discovered cooking. In the time since Lillian's father had left, housework had become for Lillian's mother a travel destination rarely reached; laundry, a friend one never remembered to call. Lillian picked up these skills by following her friends' mothers around their homes, while the mothers pretended not to notice, dropping hints about bleach or changing a vacuum bag as if it were just one more game children played. Lillian learned, and soon her home—at least the lower four and a half feet of it—developed a certain domestic routine.

But it was the cooking that occurred in her friends' homes that fascinated Lillian—the aromas that started calling to her just when she had to go home in the evening. Some smells were sharp, an olfactory clatter of heels across a hardwood floor. Others felt like the warmth in the air at the far end of summer. Lillian watched as the scent of melting cheese brought children languidly from their rooms, saw how garlic made them talkative, jokes expanding into stories of their days. Lillian thought it odd that not all mothers seemed to see it—Sarah's mother, for instance, always cooked curry when she was fighting with her teenage daughter, its smell rocketing through the house like a challenge. But Lillian soon realized that many people did not comprehend the language of smells that to Lillian was as obvious as a billboard.

Perhaps, Lillian thought, smells were for her what printed words were for others, something alive that grew and changed. Not just the smell of rosemary in the garden, but the scent on her hands after she had picked some for Elizabeth's mother, the aroma mingling with the heavy smell of chicken fat and garlic in the oven, the after-scent on the couch cushions the next day. The way, ever after, Elizabeth was always part of rosemary for Lillian, how Elizabeth's round face had crinkled up into laughter when Lillian had pushed the small, spiky branch near her nose.

Lillian liked thinking about smells, the same way she liked the weight of Mary's mother's heavy saucepan in her hands, or the way vanilla slipped into the taste of warm milk. She remembered often the time Margaret's mother had let her help with a white sauce, playing out the memory in her head the way some children try to recover, bit by detail, the moments of a favorite birthday party. Margaret had pouted, because she was, she declared stoutly, never allowed to help in the kitchen, but Lillian had ignored all twinges of loyalty and climbed up on the chair and stood, watching the butter melt across the pan like the farthest reach of a wave sinking into the sand, then the flour, at first a hideous, clumping thing destroying the image until it was stirred and stirred, Margaret's mother's hand over Lillian's on the wooden spoon when she wanted to mash the clumps, moving instead slowly, in circles, gently, until the flour-butter became smooth, smooth, until again the image was changed by the milk, the sauce expanding to contain the liquid and Lillian thought each time that the sauce could hold no more, that the sauce would break into solid and liquid, but it never did. At the last minute, Margaret's mother raised the cup of milk away from the pot, and Lillian looked at the sauce, an untouched snowfield, its smell the feeling of quiet at the end of an illness, when the world is starting to feel gentle and welcoming once again.

. . .

WHEN LILLIAN REACHED the age of eight, she began to take over the cooking in her own household. Her mother raised no objections; food had not disappeared along with Lillian's father, but while it was not impossible to cook while reading, it was problematic, and because of Lillian's mother's tendency to mis- take one spice for another if a book was unusually absorbing, meals had become less successful, if also occasionally more intriguing. All the same, the transfer of cooking duties from mother to daughter was met with a certain amount of relief on both sides.

The passing of the culinary torch marked the beginning of years of experimentation, made both slower and more unusual by Lillian's blanket refusal to engage with the printed word, even a cookbook. Learning the ins and outs of scrambled eggs, following such a pedagogical approach, could take a week— one night, plain eggs, stirred gently with a fork; the next, eggs whisked with milk; then water; then cream. If Lillian's mother objected, she made no note of it as she accompanied Lillian on her quests for ingredients, walking down the aisles reading aloud from the book of the day. Besides, Lillian thought to her- self, scrambled eggs five nights in a row seemed a fair exchange for a week otherwise dominated by James Joyce. Maybe she should add chives tonight. *Yes I said yes I will yes.*

As Lillian's skills progressed over the years, she learned other, unexpected culinary lessons. She observed how dough that was pounded made bread that was hard and moods that were equally so. She saw that cookies that were soft and warm satisfied a different human need than those that were crisp and cooled. The more she cooked, the more she began to view spices as carriers of the emotions and memories of the places they were originally from and all those they had traveled through over the years. She discovered that people seemed to react to spices much as they did to other people, relaxing instinctively into some, shivering into a kind of emotional rigor mortis when encountering others. By the time she was twelve, Lillian had begun to believe that a true cook, one who could read people and spices, could anticipate reactions before the first taste, and thus affect the way a meal or an evening would go. It was this realization that led Lillian to her Great Idea.

"I AM GOING to cook her out," Lillian told Elizabeth as they sat on her friend's front stoop.

"What?" Eight months older than Lillian, Elizabeth had long ago lost interest in cooking for a more consuming passion for the next-door neighbor, who, even as they spoke, rode and then launched his skateboard dramatically from a ramp set up in front of Elizabeth's gate.

"My mom. I'm going to cook her out."

"Lily." Elizabeth's face was a mix of scorn and sympathy. "When are you going to give up?"

"She's not as far gone as you think," said Lillian. She started to explain what she had been thinking about cookies and spices—until she realized that Elizabeth was unlikely to believe in the power of cooking and even less likely to see its potential to influence Lillian's mother.

But Lillian believed in food the way some people do religion, and thus she did what many do when faced with a critical moment in their lives. Standing that evening in the kitchen, surrounded by the pots and pans she had collected over the years, she offered up a deal.

"Let me bring her out," Lillian bargained, "and I'll cook for the rest of my life. If I can't, I'll give up cooking forever." Then she put her hand on the bottom of the fourteen-inch skillet and swore. And it was only because she was still at the tail end of twelve and largely unversed in traditional religions, that she didn't realize that most deals offered to a higher power involved sacrifice for a desired result, and thus that her risk was greater than most, as it meant winning, or losing, all.

As with many such endeavors, the beginning was a disaster. Lillian, energized by hope, charged at her mother with foods designed to knock the books right out of her hands—dishes reeking with spices that barreled straight for the stomach and emotions. For a week the kitchen was redolent with hot red peppers and cilantro. Lillian's mother ate her meals as she always did—and then retreated into a steady diet of nineteenth-century British novels, in which food rarely held a dramatic role.

And so Lillian drew back, regrouped, and gave her mother food to fit the book of the day. Porridge and tea and scones, boiled carrots and white fish. But after three months, Charles Dickens finally gave way to what appeared to be a determination on her mother's part to read the entire works of Henry James, and Lillian despaired. Her mother may have changed literary continents, but only in the most general of senses.

"She's stuck," she told Elizabeth.

"Lily, it's never going to work." Elizabeth stood in front of her mirror. "Just boil her some potatoes and be done with it."

"Potatoes," said Lillian.

A FIFTY-POUND SACK of potatoes squatted at the bottom of the steps in Lillian's basement, ordered by her mother during the *Oliver Twist* period, when staples had begun appearing at the door in such large quantities that neighbors asked Lillian if she and her mother had plans for guests, or perhaps a bomb shelter. If Lillian had been younger, she might have made a fort of food, but she was busy now. She took her knife and sliced through the burlap strings of the bag, pulling out four oblong potatoes.

"Okay, my pretties," she said.

She carried them upstairs and washed the dirt from their

waxy surfaces, using a brush to clean the dents and pockets. Elizabeth always complained when her mother made her wash the potatoes for dinner, wondering aloud to Lillian and whoever else was near why they couldn't just make a smooth potato, anyway. But Lillian liked the dips and dents, even if it meant it took more time to wash them. They reminded her of fields before they were cultivated, when every hillock or hole was a home, a scene of a small animal battle or romance.

When the potatoes were clean, she took down her favorite knife from the rack, cut them into quarters, and dropped the chunks one by one into the big blue pot full of water that she had waiting on the stove. They hit the bottom with dull, satisfying thumps, shifting about for a moment until they found their positions, then stilled, rocking only slightly as the water started to bubble.

Her mother walked into the kitchen, the *Collected Works of Henry James* in front of her face.

"Dinner or an experiment?" she asked.

"We'll see," replied Lillian.

Outside the windows, the sky was darkening. Already cars were turning on their headlights, as the light filtered gray-blue through the clouds. Inside the kitchen, the hanging lamps shone, their light reflecting off the bits of chrome, sinking quietly into the wooden countertops and floor. Lillian's mother sat down in a red-painted chair next to the kitchen table, her book open.

"*I remember,*" Lillian's mother read aloud, "*the whole begin-*

ning *as a succession of flights and drops, a little see-saw of the right throbs and the wrong.* . . ."

Lillian, listening with half an ear, bent down and took out a small pot from the cabinet. She put it on the stove and poured in milk, a third of the way up its straight sides. When she turned the dial on the stove, the flame leaped up to touch the sides of the pan.

"*There had been a moment when I believe I recognized, faint and far, the cry of a child; there had been another when I found myself starting as at the passage, before my door, of light footsteps.* . . ."

The water in the big blue pot boiled gently, the potatoes shifting about in gentle resignation like passengers on a crowded bus. The kitchen filled with the warmth of evaporated water and the smell of warming milk, while the last light came in pink through the windows. Lillian turned on the light over the stove and checked the potatoes once with the sharp end of her knife. Done. She pulled the pot from the stove and emptied the potatoes into a colander.

"Stop cooking," she said under her breath, as she ran cold water over their steaming surfaces. "Stop cooking now."

She shook the last of the water from the potatoes. The skins came off easily, like a shawl sliding off a woman's shoulders. Lillian dropped one hunk after another into the big metal bowl, then turned on the mixer and watched the chunks change from shapes to texture, mounds to lumpy clouds to cotton. Slices of butter melted in long, shining trails of yellow through the moving swirl of white. She picked up the smaller pan and slowly poured the milk into the potatoes. Then salt. Just enough.

Almost as an afterthought, she went to the refrigerator and pulled out a hard piece of Parmesan cheese. She grated some onto the cutting board, then picked up the feathery bits with her fingers and dropped them in a fine mist into the revolving bowl, where they disappeared into the mixture. She turned off the mixer, then ran her finger across the top and tasted.

"There," she said. She reached up into the cabinet and took down two pasta bowls, wide and flat, with just enough rim to hold an intricate design of blue and yellow, and placed them on the counter. Using the large wooden spoon, she scooped into the potatoes and dropped a small mountain of white in the exact center of each bowl. At the last minute, she made a small dip in the middle of each mountain, and then carefully put in an extra portion of butter.

"Mom," she said, as she carefully set the bowl and fork in front of her mother, "dinner." Lillian's mother shifted position in her chair toward the table, the book rotating in front of her body like a compass needle.

Lillian's mother's hand reached for the fork, and deftly navigated its way around the *Collected Works* and into the middle of the potatoes. She lifted the fork into the air.

"It was the first time, in a manner, that I had known space and air and freedom, all the music of summer and all the mystery of nature. And then there was consideration—and consideration was sweet. . . ."

The fork finished the journey to Lillian's mother's mouth, where it entered, then exited, clean.

"Hmmmm . . ." she said. And then all was quiet.

"I'VE GOT HER," Lillian told Elizabeth as they sat eating toast with warm peanut butter at Elizabeth's house after school.

"Because you got her to *stop* talking?" Elizabeth looked skeptical.

"You'll see," said Lillian.

Although Lillian's mother did seem calmer in the following days, the major difference was one that Lillian had not anticipated. Her mother continued to read, but now she was absolutely silent. And while Lillian, who had long ceased to see her mother's reading aloud as any attempt at communication, was not sorry to no longer be the catch-pan of treasured phrases, this was not the effect she had been hoping for. She had been certain the potatoes would be magic.

ON HER WAY home from school, Lillian took a shortcut down a narrow side street that led from the main arterial to the more rural road to her house. Halfway down the block was a small grocery store that Lillian had found when she was seven years old, on a summer afternoon when she had let go of her mother's hand in frustration and set off in a previously untraveled direction, wondering if her mother would notice her absence.

On that day years before, she had smelled the store before she saw it, hot and dusty scents tingling her nose and pulling her down the narrow street. The shop itself was tiny, perhaps the size of an apartment living room, its shelves filled with cans written in languages she didn't recognize and tall candles enclosed in glass, painted with pictures of people with halos and sad faces. A glass display case next to the cash register was filled with pans of food in bright colors—yellows and reds and greens, their smells deep and smoky, sometimes sharp.

The woman behind the counter saw Lillian standing close to the glass case, staring.

"Would you like to try?" she asked.

Not where is your mother, not how old are you, but would you like to try. Lillian looked up and smiled.

The woman reached into the case and pulled out an oblong yellow shape.

"Tamale," she said, and handed it on a small paper plate to Lillian.

The outside was soft and slightly crunchy, the inside a festival of meat, onions, tomatoes, and something that seemed vaguely like cinnamon.

"You understand food," the woman commented, nodding, as she watched Lillian eat.

Lillian looked up again, and felt herself folded into the woman's smile.

"The children call me Abuelita," she said. "I think I hear your mother coming."

Lillian listened, and heard the sound of her mother's reading voice winding its way down the alley. She cast her eyes around the store once more, and noticed an odd wooden object hanging from a hook on one of the shelves.

"What is that?" she asked, pointing.

"What do you think?" Abuelita took it down and handed it to Lillian, who looked at its irregular shape—a six-inch-long stick with a rounded bulb on one end with ridges carved into it like furrows in a field.

"I think it is a magic wand," Lillian responded.

"Perhaps," said Abuelita. "Perhaps you should keep it, just in case."

Lillian took the wand and slid it into her coat pocket like a spy palming a secret missive.

"Come back anytime, little cook," Abuelita said.

Lillian had returned to the store often over the years. Abuelita had taught her about spices and foods she never encountered in Elizabeth's or Margaret's houses. There was avocado, wrinkled and grumpy on the outside, green spring within, creamy as ice cream when smashed into guacamole. There were the smoky flavors of chipotle peppers and the sharp-sweet crunch of cilantro, which Lillian loved so much Abuelita would always give her a sprig to eat as she walked home. Abuelita didn't talk a lot, but when she did, it was conversation.

So when Lillian walked into the store, a week after making mashed potatoes for her mother, Abuelita looked at her closely for a moment.

"You are missing something," she noted after a moment.

"It didn't work," Lillian replied, despairingly. "I thought I had her, but it didn't work."

"Tell me," said Abuelita simply, and Lillian did, about cookies and spices and Henry James and mashed potatoes and her feeling that perhaps, in the end, food would not be the magic that would wake her mother from her long, literary sleep, that perhaps in the end, sleep was all there was for her mother.

After Lillian ended her story, Abuelita was quiet for a while. "It's not that what you did was wrong; it's just that you aren't finished."

"What else am I supposed to do?"

"Lillian, each person's heart breaks in its own way. Every cure will be different—but there are some things we all need. Before anything else, we need to feel safe. You did that for her."

"So why is she still gone?"

"Because to be a part of this world, we need more than safety. Your mother needs to remember what she lost and want it again.

"I have an idea," Abuelita said. "This may take a few minutes."

Abuelita handed Lillian a warm corn tortilla and motioned for her to sit at the small round table that stood next to the front door. As Lillian watched, Abuelita tore off the back panel from a small brown paper bag and wrote on it, her forehead furrowing in concentration.

"I am not a writer," she commented as she finished. "I never thought it was worth much. But you will get the idea."

She put down the paper, picked up another small grocery bag, and began gathering items off the store shelves, her back to Lillian. Then she folded the paper, placed it in the top of the bag, and held the bag out to Lillian.

"Here," she said, "let me know how it goes."

AT HOME, Lillian opened the bag and inhaled aromas of orange, cinnamon, bittersweet chocolate, and something she couldn't quite identify, deep and mysterious, like perfume lingering in the folds of a cashmere scarf. She emptied the ingredients from the bag onto the kitchen counter and unfolded the paper Abuelita had placed on top, looking at it with a certain reserve. It was a recipe, even if this one was in Abuelita's writing, each letter thick as a branch and almost as stiff. Lillian's hand itched to throw the recipe away—but she hesitated as her eyes caught on the first line of the instructions.

Find your magic wand.

Lillian stopped.

"Well, okay, then," she said. She pulled a chair up to the kitchen counter and stood on it, reaching on top of the cabinet for the small, red tin box where she kept her most valued possessions.

The wand was close to the bottom of the box, underneath her first movie ticket and the miniature replica of a Venetian bridge her father had given her not long before he departed, leaving behind only money and his smell on the sheets, the latter gone long before Lillian learned how to do laundry. Underneath the wand was an old photograph of her mother holding a baby Lillian, her mother's eyes looking directly into the camera, her smile as huge and rich and gorgeous as any chocolate cake Lillian could think of making.

Lillian gazed at the photograph for a long time, then got down off the chair, the wand gripped in her right hand, and picked up the recipe.

Put milk in a saucepan. Use real milk, the thick kind.

Abuelita was always complaining about the girls from Lillian's school who wouldn't eat her tamales, or who asked for enchiladas without sour cream and then carefully peeled off the cheese from the outside.

"Skinny girls," Abuelita would say with disdain, "they think you attract bees with a stick."

Make orange curls. Set aside.

Lillian smiled. She felt about her zester the way some women do about a pair of spiky red shoes—a frivolous splurge, good only for parties, but oh so lovely. The day Lillian had found the little utensil at a garage sale a year before, she had brought it to Abuelita, face shining. She didn't even know what it was for back then, she just knew she loved its slim stainless-steel handle, the fanciful bit of metal at the working end with its five demure little holes, the edge scalloped around the openings like frills on a petticoat. There were so few occasions for a zester; using it felt like a holiday.

Lillian picked up the orange and held it to her nose, breathing in. It smelled of sunshine and sticky hands, shiny green leaves and blue, cloudless skies. An orchard, somewhere— California? Florida?—her parents looking at each other over the top of her head, her mother handing her a yellow-orange fruit, bigger than Lillian's two hands could hold, laughing, telling her "this is where grocery stores come from."

Now Lillian took the zester and ran it along the rounded outer surface of the fruit, slicing the rind into five long orange curls, leaving behind the bitter white beneath it.

Break the cinnamon in half.

The cinnamon stick was light, curled around itself like a brittle roll of papyrus. Not a stick at all, Lillian remembered as she looked closer, but bark, the meeting place between inside and out. It crackled as she broke it, releasing a spiciness, part heat, part sweet, that pricked at her eyes and nose, and made her tongue tingle without even tasting it.

Add orange peel and cinnamon to milk. Grate the chocolate.

The hard, round cake of chocolate was wrapped in yellow plastic with red stripes, shiny and dark when she opened it. The chocolate made a rough sound as it brushed across the fine section of the grater, falling in soft clouds onto the counter, releasing a scent of dusty back rooms filled with bittersweet chocolate and old love letters, the bottom drawers of antique desks and the last leaves of autumn, almonds and cinnamon and sugar.

Into the milk it went.

Add anise.

Such a small amount of ground spice in the little bag Abuelita had given her. It lay there quietly, unremarkable, the color of wet beach sand. She undid the tie around the top of the bag and swirls of warm gold and licorice danced up to her nose, bringing with them miles of faraway deserts and a dark, starless sky, a longing she could feel in the back of her eyes, her fingertips. Lillian knew, putting the bag back down on the counter, that the spice was more grown-up than she was.

Really, Abuelita? she asked into the air.

Just a touch. Let it simmer until it all comes together. You'll know when it does.

Lillian turned the heat on low. She went to the refrigerator, got the whipping cream, and set the mixer on high, checking the saucepan periodically. After a while, she could see the specks of chocolate disappearing into the milk, melting, becoming thicker, creamier, one thing rather than many.

Use your wand.

Lillian picked up the wand, rolling the handle musingly between the palms of her hands. She gripped the slender central stick with purpose and dipped the ridged end into the pan. Rolling the wand forward and back between her palms, she sent the ridges whirling through the liquid, sending the milk and chocolate across the pan in waves, creating bubbles across the top of the surface.

"Abracadabra," she said. "Please."

Now add to your mother's coffee.

One life skill Lillian's mother had not abandoned for books was making coffee; a pot was always warm on the counter, as dependable as a wool coat. Lillian filled her mother's mug halfway with coffee, then added the milk chocolate, holding back the orange peels and cinnamon so the liquid would be smooth across the tongue.

Top with whipping cream, for softness. Give to your mother.

"What is that amazing smell?" her mother asked, as Lillian carried the cup into the living room.

"Magic," Lillian said.

Her mother reached for the cup and raised it to her mouth, blowing gently across the surface, the steam spiraling up to meet her nose. She sipped tentatively, almost puzzled, her eyes looking up from her book to stare at something far away, her face flushing slightly. When she was finished, she handed the cup back to Lillian.

"Where did you learn to make that?" she said, leaning back and closing her eyes.

"THAT'S WONDERFUL," said Abuelita when Lillian recounted the story to her the next day. "You made her remember her life. Now she just needs to reach out to it. That recipe," Abuelita said in answer to Lillian's questioning face, "must be yours. But you will find it," she continued. "You are a cook. It's a gift from your mother."

Lillian raised an eyebrow skeptically. Abuelita gazed at her, gently amused.

"Sometimes, *niña*, our greatest gifts grow from what we are not given."

Two days later, Lillian headed straight home after classes. The weather had turned during the night, and the air as Lillian left school that day had a clear, brittle edge to it. Lillian walked at a fast pace, to match the air around her. She lived at the edge of town, where a house could still stand next door to a small orchard, and where kitchen gardens served as reminders of larger farms not so long gone. There was one orchard she particularly liked, a grove of apple trees, twisted and leaning, growing toward each other like old cousins. The owner was as old as his trees and wasn't able to take care of them much anymore. Grass grew thick around their bases and ivy was beginning to grasp its way up their trunks. But the apples seemed not to have noticed the frailty of their source, and were firm and crisp and sweet; Lillian waited for them every year, and for the smile of the old man as he handed them to her across the fence.

He was in among the trees when she walked by and called out to him. He turned and squinted in her direction. He waved, then turned and reached up into one of the trees, checking first one apple then the next. Finally satisfied, he came toward her, an apple in each hand.

"Here," he said, handing them to her. "A taste of the new season."

THE SKY WAS already darkening by the time Lillian got home, and the cold air came in the door with her. Her mother sat in her usual chair in the living room, a book held under a circle of light made by the reading lamp.

"I have something for you, Mom," Lillian said, and placed one of the apples in her mother's hand.

Lillian's mother took the apple and absentmindedly pressed its smooth, cold surface against her cheek.

"It feels like fall," she commented, and bit into it. The sharp, sweet sound of the crunch filled the air like a sudden burst of applause and Lillian laughed at the noise. Her mother looked up, smiling at the sound, and her eyes met her daughter's.

"Why, Lillian," she said, her voice rippling with surprise, "look how you've grown."

Claire

R eally, Claire thought, some exits you needed to practice
  ahead of time. She stood with her husband and children
in the doorway, her three-year-old daughter gripping her leg
like an octopus with bones, the baby screaming in rage as he
attempted to climb over James's shoulder to get to his mother.

"What do I do if he won't take his bottle?" James dodged
small hands as they grasped for leverage on his nose.

"Give him the bunny." Bunny, bunny, magical bunny, with
ears whose tips just fit inside a baby's mouth, and fur as soft as
flower petals.

"Bunny? I thought it was his blanket."

"That was weeks ago." Claire leaned down and began to
dislodge her daughter's fingers. "Now it's the bunny."

"Where are you going, Mommy?" her daughter asked, tightening her grip. "It's dark outside."

"Mommy's just going out for a little while," Claire told her soothingly.

"Don't go," her daughter said, beginning to cry. The baby, furious at the interruption, ramped up his volume.

"Lucy, Mommy's going to learn how to cook," James interjected above the noise. "That'll be fun, won't it?"

"You don't have . . . to . . . cook . . . peanut butter."

"Oh, but Mommy is going to learn how to cook noodles and bread and yum, maybe even fish," James added enthusiastically.

Claire tensed. Lucy's fear of the dark had only recently been mitigated by the acquisition of a friendly band of tetras that swam in the glow of an aquarium near her bed.

"Mommy is going to cook fish?"

"No, no, of course not," Claire soothed, taking refuge in her ignorance, because, she realized, she didn't actually know. The cooking class wasn't even her idea; it was a gift from her mother, one she still wasn't sure if she was offended or intrigued by.

As Lucy looked up, uncertain whether to believe her mother or not, Claire took advantage of her daughter's distraction to release herself and sprint for the car. She drove, waving in earnest cheeriness, to the end of the block and pulled over, shaking.

"You can do this," she told herself. "You have a college degree. You can leave your house and go to a cooking class."

She smelled something and looked down at her shirt. The baby had spit up on her collar. She grabbed a wadded Kleenex from the seat next to her, spat on it, and scrubbed at the residue.

THE COOKING CLASS was held in a restaurant named Lillian's, on the main street of town, almost hidden by a front garden dense with ancient cherry trees, roses, and the waving spikes and soft mounds of green herbs. Set between the straight lines of a bank and the local movie theater, the restaurant was oddly incongruous, a moment of lush colors and gently moving curves, like an affair in the midst of an otherwise orderly life. Passersby often reached out to run their hands along the tops of the lavender bushes that stretched luxuriantly above the cast-iron fence, the soft, dusty scent remaining on their fingers for hours after.

Those who entered the gate and followed the winding brick path through the garden discovered an Arts and Crafts house whose front rooms had been converted into a dining area. There were no more than ten tables in all, each table's personality defined by nearby architectural elements, one nestled into a bay window, another engaged in companionable conversation with a built-in bookshelf. Some tables had views of the garden, while others, hidden like secrets in the darker, protected corners of the room, held their patrons' attention within the edges of their tabletops.

Outside, heavy wooden chairs lined the front porch, ready

for overflow customers. The chairs were always full, not only because of the food, but because the restaurant staff seemed to take an almost perverse pride in never rushing anyone through a meal. First come, first served. And served, and served, muttered some patrons as they observed the length of the wait list; but they always stayed, settling into the deep Adirondack chairs with glasses of red wine, until waiting became a social event of its own and parties of two melded into four and six, which of course sped up nothing at all.

That was how it worked at Lillian's—nothing ever went quite the way you planned. The menu would change without notice, disconcerting those who craved familiarity, yet who later admitted that the meal they ended up eating was somehow exactly what they had wanted. And while the restaurant's subtle lighting gave it an aura of peacefulness and its infinite wine list seemed destined for special occasions, evenings, no matter how carefully orchestrated, often detoured in surprising directions—a proposal veering into a breakup that left both parties stunned and relieved, a business meeting smoldering into a passionate grope session by the recycling bins in the back.

Claire had been to the restaurant twice—the first time almost eight years earlier with a man replete with success, who saw in Claire's sleek golden hair and heart-shaped face a moment he had not experienced. Over the weeks, his appearances at her bank window had become so numerous that Nancy, who doled out traveler's checks the next window over, remarked that he had better ask Claire out before he was made an honorary employee. Claire, who was beginning to feel that her most passionate relationship was with her cell phone provider, made the first move, resting her hand on the bills as she passed them under the partition that divided her from her suitor.

He was, Claire acknowledged, a charming enough date, erudite and well informed; at dinner he ordered the wine with the comfortable air of someone inviting an old friend to the table. And yet it was strange. His fish was perfectly cooked—Claire knew because he had fed her a bite, leaning across the table as if reaching her mouth was the final challenge in the great quest of his life—and yet the odor of fish stayed with him afterward, reminding her of high school nights spent under the piers at the beach with boys she no longer remembered or wanted to. When he tried to kiss her as they walked down the street after dinner, she noticed a new model car and turned quickly to point it out.

Claire's second visit to Lillian's restaurant was two years later, with James. Claire had hesitated, remembering the fish-date debacle, and yet by then she was so infatuated with James that it didn't matter. The ring James gave her, before the wine or food had even arrived, slid onto her finger like his hands moving across her skin. They toasted with water and drank their champagne later, in bed.

TONIGHT, the restaurant was dark. Claire wondered if perhaps she had the wrong night, after all. Maybe she had missed the class and could go home now. James would need help with the baby. She knew from experience that the baby could cry for hours, refusing the bottles of pumped milk with the incredu-lous air of a gold club member told he had to fly coach. In the midst of all the noise, their daughter might well be forgotten, and Claire suddenly remembered Lucy's newly acquired inter-est in haircuts.

Behind her, on the other side of the gate, Claire could hear people talking as they walked toward the movie theater. She looked over her shoulder, watching them pass. When she looked forward again, she saw a glow coming from the back of the res-taurant, illuminating a narrow stone pathway that led around the side.

The gate creaked behind her and an older couple walked up to Claire.

"Are you going in, too?" the woman asked, smiling.

"Yes," said Claire, and she began to make her way carefully along the stones to the back door.

THE KITCHEN WAS a blast of light after the darkness of the garden. Stainless-steel counters framed the room, heavy iron pasta pots hung from hooks next to copper sauté pans, while knives stuck to magnetic strips along the walls like swords in an armory. A line was forming at a cavernous metal sink where other students were washing their hands—a girl-woman whose eyes were ringed with black eyeliner, a young man with glasses and sandy-colored hair.

When it was her turn, Claire washed her hands conscientiously, the soap popping and foaming between her fingers. She wondered if she should wash all the way to her elbows, like a surgeon, but the line was growing behind her. Claire wiped her hands on a paper towel and walked over to the trash can where the older man she had met outside greeted her with a nod.

"Do you mind?" he said, smiling, his hand reaching toward her shoulder. She looked at him questioningly.

"Just a bit of tissue," he said, brushing deftly at the collar of her shirt. "Have to do that all the time for my wife—we've got four grandchildren." He dropped the paper towel in the trash can and held out his hand. "My name's Carl."

THE STUDENTS WERE finding their way to the chairs, set up in two rows of four facing a big wooden prep table with a mirror suspended over it. Carl and his wife were settling in at the far end of the second row; Claire started in their direction, but saw a beautiful woman with olive skin and eyes the color of melted chocolate tentatively taking the chair next to them. In the chair beside her, almost hidden in the corner of the room, sat a man whose sadness seemed to have been pressed into his shirt.

Claire took a chair in the front row, next to a fragile-looking older woman with silver hair and bright blue eyes, whose fingers played absentmindedly with a purple pen. From her seat, Claire scanned her fellow students, looking for personalities, relationships. Carl and his wife were together, but as far as Claire could tell, the seats were otherwise filled with people seemingly unhooked from—or in some cases more likely never hooked to—partners.

Looking about, Claire realized that she knew nothing of the people around her, and they knew exactly as much about her. The strangeness of it caught her. It was hard to remember the last time she had gone anywhere without her children, or her husband. Even those few times, she had been with people who knew her as a member of a nuclear family, a role as much a part of her identity as the color of her hair or the shape of her hands. When was the last time she had been someplace where no one knew who she was?

She wondered what her family was doing at home, if the baby had taken his bottle, if James was rubbing Lucy's back as she went to sleep. Would he remember to move his hand in clockwise circles? Would he know that the baby always kicked off his blanket, and go back in and cover him up?

How strange, she thought. These people here, they looked at her and thought she was alone, she whose children were with her even in her dreams.

"My name is Lillian. Welcome to the School of Essential Ingredients." The woman stood behind the wooden counter, facing the students in their chairs. Her eyes were calm, her smooth, dark hair held loosely together at the base of her neck; Claire guessed she was probably thirty-five years old, just a few years older than Claire herself. Claire watched Lillian's hands move gently across the utensils and pots on the counter as she talked, like a mother playing with her child's curls.

"The first question people always ask me is, What are the essential ingredients?" Lillian paused and smiled. "I might as well tell you, there isn't a list and I've never had one. Nor do I hand out recipes. All I can say is that you will learn what you need to, and you should feel free to write down whatever comes to mind during class.

"We'll meet once a month, always on Mondays, when the restaurant is closed. You're welcome to come to the restaurant on other nights and learn by eating what others are cooking, but on the first Monday of the month the kitchen is yours.

"Everybody ready?" The class nodded obediently.

"Well then, I think we'll start with the beginning." Lillian turned and walked to the back door. She walked outside, letting in a draft of air, and returned carrying a large Styrofoam cooler in her arms. Claire could hear its contents clattering softly. She looked at the box, then around the room. In the back, Carl smiled and whispered to his wife, who nodded.

"Crabs," said Lillian.

The older woman with the blue eyes leaned toward Claire. "Well, that's starting off with a bang," she commented dryly.

Lillian lifted the lid and drew out one of the creatures. Its shell was the color of dried blood, with black pea eyes perched on the front edge. Its antennae shivered, reaching out for input, and its front pincers waved, ludicrously out of proportion to both its body and the situation, as it searched for air in an ocean of oxygen.

"Are we going to kill them?" asked the black-eyeliner girl.

"Yes, we are, Chloe. It is the first, most essential lesson." Lillian's expression was quiet, calm. "If you think about it," she went on, "every time we prepare food we interrupt a life cycle. We pull up a carrot or kill a crab—or maybe just stop the mold that's growing on a wedge of cheese. We make meals with those ingredients and in doing so we give life to something else. It's a basic equation, and if we pretend it doesn't exist, we're likely to miss the other important lesson, which is to give respect to both sides of the equation. So we start here.

"Have any of you caught your own crabs?" Lillian asked the group. In the back, Carl raised his hand.

"Then you know," Lillian nodded toward him. "There are rules about which crabs we can keep. Here in the Northwest, your crab needs to measure at least six inches across the back of the shell and we only keep the males—you can tell which are the males because they have a skinny triangle on their abdomen, while the females have a wider one."

"Why just the males?" said the young man with the sandy hair.

"The females are the breeders," Lillian answered. "You

always need to take care of the breeders." Her smile landed, just for a flicker of time, on Claire. Claire surreptitiously checked her collar, which was clean.

"Now, when I'm deciding which ingredients to put together, I like to think about the central element in the dish. What flavors would it want? So I want you to think about crabs. Close your eyes. What comes to mind?"

Claire obediently lowered her eyelids, feeling her lashes brush against her skin. She thought of the fine hairs on the sides of a crab's body, the way they moved in the water. She thought of the sharp edges of claws moving their way across the wavy sand bed of the sea, of water so pervasive it was air as well as liquid.

"Salt," she said aloud, surprising herself.

"Good, now keep going," Lillian prompted. "What might we do to contrast or bring out the flavor?"

"Garlic," added Carl, "maybe some red pepper flakes."

"And butter," said Chloe, "lots of butter."

There was a general murmur of appreciation.

"Okay, then," Lillian said, "let's break you into groups and have you learn with your hands."

CLAIRE'S GROUP STOOD at one of the big metal sinks. Four crabs skittered about, their antennae quivering as they encountered the hard surface.

The man with the sandy hair came to stand next to Claire at the sink. She looked up and saw that he was watching her, smiling. She stopped, startled, recognizing an expression of casual male appraisal suddenly made visible because it had long been absent. When was the last time that had happened, Claire wondered.

It was all so very strange, she thought, being here. An hour earlier she had been with her children, the smell of their shampoo, their skin, mingling with hers until it became her own scent. She had sat in the big red chair in the living room, nursing her son and reading to her daughter, who had crawled in next to her and was playing with the buttons on her sleeve.

She had never been touched so much in her life, never felt so much skin against her own. And yet, since she had become a mother it was as if her body had become invisible to anyone but her children. When was the last time someone she didn't know had looked at her as if she was . . . what? A possibility.

She remembered being pregnant, holding the quivering secret of the baby inside her. Her sensuality lay upon her, sweet and heavy as tropical air. Her hips, widening to accommodate the growing baby, swung when she walked and her skin felt every texture, every touch, until she craved James's homecoming each night.

But as the skin across her stomach tightened and expanded she developed a new identity. "Can I?" strangers would ask, reaching toward her, as if her stomach was a charm that would change their fortune, their lives. And yet—"You are asking if you can touch *me*," she wanted to tell them. But she understood that that wasn't what they were saying at all.

Then, after the children were born, it was as if no one could see further than the soft hair, the round cheeks of the babies she carried. She became the frame for the picture that was her son and daughter. Which was fine with her, Claire thought; the babies were beautiful and she was all too ready to forget her own body, which had ballooned and shrunk and which she had no time to do anything about anyway. When men did smile at her, it was with safe, benign smiles, filled with neither hope nor interest.

"You are out of circulation, honey," Claire's older sister had told her, "you might as well get used to it."

James was the one person who still saw her in the old light; he wanted the love life they'd had before children, didn't understand why, at the end of the day, she didn't want him. When he'd reach for her, after she had finished nursing the baby to sleep and was finally, finally, on her way to shower off the day, all she could think was, "Not you, too?" She couldn't tell him; it seemed too awful, but he seemed to sense it anyway and after a while he stopped trying.

Standing there by the chopping block, Claire realized that she was being looked at by a man she didn't know, for the first time in years. It wasn't an unqualified success of an experience, she thought wryly, as she realized that the sandy-haired man's gaze had moved beyond her to halt, with an air of dumbstruck infatuation, on the woman with the olive skin and brown eyes—and yet it was exciting in its own way to be visible, Claire thought, to be tossed back with the other breeders. She had thought she was past all that, thought the needs of her children's two small bodies fulfilled all of hers.

"How ARE WE DOING over here?" Lillian came up next to Carl at the sink.

"We're ready for the boiling water," said the man with the sandy hair.

"I know a lot of people use boiling water, but I do it differently," Lillian explained. "It's a little harder on you, but it's easier for the crab, and the meat has a more elegant taste if it's cleaned before it's cooked." Lillian reached into the sink and smoothly picked up one of the crustaceans from behind, its front pincers flailing like a drunk in slow motion. She laid the crab belly-side down on the chopping block.

"If you're going to do it this way, it's better for both you and the crab if you are decisive." She placed two fingers on the back of the crab for a quiet moment, then gripped her long, slim fingers under the back end of the crab's upper shell and gave a quick jerk, like a carpenter ripping a wooden shingle from a roof. The armored covering came off in her hand and the crab lay open on the block, the exposed interior a mixture of gray and dark yellow.

"Now," she said, "you take a sharp knife." She picked up

a heavy, square-shaped cleaver, "and you do this." The cleaver came down with a sharp thump, and the crab's body lay in two symmetrical pieces, legs moving feebly. Claire stared.

"It's okay," Lillian said, as she carefully picked up the body and walked to the sink, "the crab is dead now."

"Perhaps we should tell that to its legs," Carl commented, smiling sympathetically at Claire's expression.

Lillian gently ran water over the crab's interior, her fingers working through the yellow and gray.

"What . . . ?" said Claire, pointing at the gray sickle shapes that were falling into the sink.

"Lungs," replied Lillian. "They're beautiful, in a way. They feel a little like magnolia petals."

"If you want the sauce to seep into the meat, you'll need to crack the shells of the legs," Lillian added. "It'll work better if you do this." She brought the crab back to the chopping block and took the cleaver once again; she made a quick, decisive cut between each of the legs, leaving the crab in ten pieces, then took the side of the cleaver and cracked each piece with a solid, rocking motion.

"I know," Lillian said, "it's a lot to take in. But what we are doing has the virtue of being honest—you aren't just opening a can and pretending the crabmeat came from nowhere. And when you're honest about what you are doing, I find care and respect follow more easily.

"Now I'll leave you to try."

The man with the sandy hair looked at Claire. "My name's

Ian," he volunteered. "If you want to clean, I can do this part. I mean, if it makes you nervous."

Claire looked past Ian and saw that Carl's wife had picked up a crab and was putting it on the chopping block. The two women looked at each other. Carl's wife nodded, then reso-lutely reached down, scooped the underside of the shell, and pulled it off the body. She looked at Claire.

"You can do it," she said.

Claire turned to Ian. "No, thank you," she replied, "I'm going to try this myself." She walked over to the sink and picked up a crab. It was lighter than she had imagined, the underside of the shell oddly soft and fragile. She took a breath and put the crab down on the butcher block, facing away from her. Clos-ing her eyes she slid her fingers under the side of the shell. The edges were knobby, cool against her skin. She gripped the shell and pulled. Nothing happened. She clenched her teeth against the thought of what she was doing and yanked again. With a wrenching sound, the shell came off in her hand.

"Give me the cleaver," she said to Ian. With a sharp whack, she cut the crab in two. She walked over to the sink, her hands shaking.

THE LEATHERY PETALS of the crab's lungs came loose between Claire's fingers and flowed away with the cold water. As she stood at the sink, Claire's body was shivering and yet—and this ran counter to everything she thought about herself—deeply stirred. It was like jumping off the high diving board when you believed you couldn't, hitting the cold water and feeling it fly over your hot skin. Claire the bank teller, Claire the mother, would never have killed a crab. But then again, Claire thought, these days she was a lot of things she didn't recognize.

When exactly had she become the human bundling board in her own bed, Claire wondered. She didn't know. Well, no, that wasn't true—she did know. The first time she held her daughter and their bodies curled into each other. The forty-fifth time she read *Goodnight Moon*; the morning James touched her breast and teasingly told their nursing son, "Remember, those are mine," and she wondered when those breasts, whose firm and luxurious weight she had loved to hold in her own hands, had ceased in any way to be hers.

How could she explain to James what it was like—he who left the house every morning and cut the physical tie with his children with the apparent ease of someone slipping off a pair of shoes? He was still separate—a condition she viewed with anger or jealousy, depending on the day—and she was not.

When they were in bed at night and she felt James turn away in resignation, a movement as heavy as the flipping of a stone slab, she wanted to yell that she did remember, she did. She remembered watching James's mouth long before she knew his name, imagining her finger along the smooth upper curve of his ears, her tongue traveling the hills and valleys of his knuckles. She remembered the shock of their first kiss, although they had known it was coming for days, moving toward each other slowly until it seemed there was no space left and yet still it was a surprise, how suddenly her life shifted, how certain she was that she would do anything as long as it meant she didn't have to move her lips, her tongue, her body away from James's, whose curves and rhythms matched her own until it didn't matter that they were right outside her apartment and the keys were in her hand, thirty seconds was too long to stop.

She remembered his long fingers slipping lower on her waist as they danced at her younger sister's wedding. The backyard as the sprinklers ran and the neighbors had a party next door and she had rolled on top of him while the water fell on her hair. The endless winter mornings in bed as the gray light slowly brightened and James caressed her bulging belly and assured her she was the sexiest woman he had ever seen. She remembered, she did. They were the memories she played in her head these days as she soothed herself to sleep, long after his breathing told her it was safe.

It wasn't just that she was a mother now, or in need of some good lingerie, as her younger sister had recommended. She realized, standing there at the sink, that when she replayed those scenes in her head, she was trying to find someone she had lost, and it wasn't James. James was still the same.

"THAT'S PROBABLY CLEAN NOW." Carl's wife was standing next to her. "My name is Helen, by the way."

"Mine's Claire."

"Carl tells me you're a mother."

"Yes—I have a three-year-old and a baby." Claire, lost for the moment in her thoughts of James, remembered her children with a start.

"That's an interesting time," Helen replied carefully.

"It is," Claire responded, then paused. Something in Helen's expression, an openness, a sense of listening, made Claire feel bolder. "I love them," she said. "Sometimes, though, I wonder . . ."

"Who you are without them?" Helen offered with a gentle smile.

"Yes," Claire said gratefully.

They walked back to the chopping block, Claire carrying the crab in her hands. Helen paused. "You know, I'd like to ask you something a friend asked me once, if you don't think it's too personal."

"What is it?"

"What do you do that makes you happy? Just you."

Claire looked at Helen for a moment and thought, the crab resting on the block beneath her hands.

"I was just wondering," Helen continued. "No one ever

asked me when I was your age, and I think it's a good thing to think about."

Claire nodded. Then she took the cleaver and cut the crab into ten pieces.

WHAT DID SHE DO that made her happy? The question implied action, a conscious purpose. She did many things in a day, and many things made her happy, but that, Claire could tell, wasn't the issue. Nor the only one, Claire realized. Because in order to consciously do something that made you happy, you'd have to know who you were. Trying to figure that out these days was like fishing on a lake on a moonless night—you had no idea what you would get.

On the morning she had gone into labor with Lucy, Claire had walked about their garden, holding the hose over the rose-bushes, one contraction per rosebush, ten minutes, five. The pains were slow and warm at first, like menstrual cramps. It was a gorgeous Sunday and all around her people were work-ing on their yards, lawn mowers buzzing in preparation for backyard barbecues and pitchers of Sunday sangría. She felt completely and utterly herself, a woman about to give birth.

Over the hours, the labor pains had sharpened. When they arrived at the hospital, time changed and nurses moved with quick precision, strapping monitors onto her and plugging her into machines. Everything was gray and cold, except for the pain that began to grind into her, deeper and deeper, pulling her under. She kept thinking the waves would slow or break for a moment, but they didn't, one after another until there was nowhere left to go but in, to dive down and hope for air on the other side, but there was no air, no way out, just a desperate reaching and grasping until finally she felt something deep inside her—not physical, not emotional, simply her—break into pieces. And into the arms of that cracked-apart person that had been Claire, they placed a baby and a love came out of her, through the pieces, that she didn't even know was possible.

She remembered thinking later, as she held her newborn child in the cool darkness of her hospital room, that all she would need was one quiet moment and she would be able to find those pieces of herself and put them back the way they had been. It wouldn't be too hard. But the quiet moment hadn't happened, lost between feedings and laundry and a newfound belief that any need of hers fell naturally second to her daughter's. Over time, the pieces had found new places, not where they had been but where they could be, until the person she became was someone she barely recognized. She didn't necessarily like that person, and it stunned her that James either couldn't or wouldn't see, was willing to sleep with someone who wasn't really her. It felt—but she didn't know how she could ever explain this to him—as if he were cheating on her.

. . .

ONCE THE CRABS were cleaned, Lillian explained that they were going to be roasted in the oven. "We'll make a sauce, and it will permeate into the meat through the cracks in the shell. The best way to eat it is with your hands."

The class reassembled in their seats facing the wooden counter in the middle of the room. Lillian put out ingredients— sticks of butter, mounds of chopped onion and minced ginger and garlic, a bottle of white wine, pepper, lemons.

"We'll melt the butter first," she explained, "and then cook the onions until they become translucent." The class could hear the small snaps as the onions met the hot surface. "Make sure the butter doesn't brown, though," Lillian cautioned, "or it will taste burned."

When the pieces of onion began to disappear into the butter, Lillian quickly added the minced ginger, a new smell, part kiss, part playful slap. Garlic came next, a soft, warm cushion under the ginger, followed by salt and pepper.

"You can add some red pepper flakes, if you like," Lillian said, "and more or less garlic or ginger or other ingredients, depending on the mood you're in or the one you want to create. Now," she continued, "we'll coat the crab and roast it in the oven.

"Carl, could you help me out?" Lillian handed a bottle of white wine to Carl, who pulled the cork with the skill of years of celebrations and dinners. "White wine is perfect with crab."

Lillian poured the wine into a set of glasses and motioned to Claire. "Could you pass these around?"

One by one Claire carried the glasses to the members of the class—Carl and Helen, Ian, the woman with the beautiful brown eyes, the sad young man, Chloe with the black eyeliner, the woman with the silver hair who smiled absently as if perhaps she knew Claire. Claire returned to her seat.

"Now," Lillian said, "what I'd like you to do is relax. Listen. Be still. Smell the change in the air as the crab cooks. Don't worry; I'll give you time to get to know one another later, but for right now, I want you to concentrate on your senses."

Claire closed her eyes. The room around her quieted as the students placed notepads on the floor and settled into comfortable positions. Claire's breathing deepened, filling her lungs, slowing her heart. She felt her shoulder blades slide down the lines of her back and her chin rise, as if to bring the air more easily into her nose. The fragrance of the warming ingredients drifted across the room, seeping into her skin, scents both mellow and intriguing, like the lazy excitement of a finger running down the inside of your arm. When Claire lifted her glass to her lips, the white wine erased the other sensations in a clean, cool wave, only to allow them to return again.

"I've warmed some wine and fresh lemon juice," Lillian noted, "to add at the last minute." Claire felt the heat from the oven as the door opened and shut, heard the sizzling of the sauce on the crabs, sensed the flavors intensify and change as Lillian added the crisp, clear elements of white wine and lemon.

55

"Okay, you can open your eyes. Come and eat." Claire stood up and moved toward the counter with the other students. They stood one another, shoulders gently jostling, and reached into the pan, gingerly taking out pieces of crab and dropping them onto the small plates Lillian had waiting.

"This is incredible, Carl," Claire heard Helen exclaim softly next to her. "Try a piece." Helen raised her dripping fingers to Carl's mouth and fed him a bite. She turned to Claire.

"Have you tried any yet?"

Claire shook her head. "It's awfully hot, still."

Helen deftly pulled a piece of meat from the shell. She smiled when she saw Claire's amazement.

"Asbestos fingers, dear. From years of taking fish sticks from the oven. There are a few benefits. Now, forget all that and eat."

"Hmmm," Claire responded, and lifted the crab to her mouth, closing her eyes one more time, shutting out the room around her. The meat touched her tongue and the taste ran through her, full and rich and complicated, dense as a long, deep kiss. She took another bite and felt her feet settle into the floor and the rest of her flow into a river of ginger and garlic and lemon and wine. She stood, even when that bite, and the next and the next were gone, feeling the river wind its way to her fingers, her toes, her belly, the base of her spine, melting all the pieces of her into something warm and golden. She breathed in, and in that one, quiet moment felt herself come back together again.

Slowly, Claire opened her eyes.

Carl

C arl and Helen came to the cooking class together. They were one of those couples that seemed to have been born within close proximity to each other, twins of a nonbiological origin. Nothing physical substantiated the thought; he was tall and tended toward thin, with astonishingly white hair and clear blue eyes, while Helen was shorter, rounder, smiling easily with the other students in the class, pulling out pictures of her grandchildren, with the natural understanding that ice must be broken and babies do it better than most things. And yet, even when Carl and Helen were separated by the width of the room, you thought of them as standing next to each other, both heads nodding intently in response to whatever was being said or done.

It was unusual to see a couple at Lillian's cooking school;

the classes were expensive enough that most couples sent a designated representative—Marco Polo–like explorers on a marital mission to bring back new spices, tricks to change meals or lives. As elected delegates, they usually arrived with clearly defined goals—one-pot dinners for busy families, a never-miss pasta sauce—occasionally undermined by the lush solidity of fresh goat cheese lingering on the tongue, a red-wine marinade left for days to insinuate itself into a flank of steak. Life at home was rarely the same afterward.

When a couple came to class together, it meant something else entirely—food as a solution, a diversion, or, occasionally, a playground. Lillian was always curious. Would they divide their functions or pass tasks back and forth? Did they touch each other as they did the food? Lillian sometimes wondered why psychologists focused so much on a couple's life in their bedroom. You could learn everything about a couple just watching the kitchen choreography as they prepared dinner.

In the swirl of before-class socializing, Carl and Helen stood together at one side of the room, watching those around them, their hands gently linked. Her face was smooth, in marked contrast to her white hair; he stood taller for being next to her, his eyes kind behind wire-rimmed glasses. There was no sense of remove to their position, no seeming desire for isolation; they seemed to exist in an eddy of calm that drew others, women first, toward them.

"Oh, no"—Helen laughed, talking to the young woman with olive skin and large brown eyes who had approached them—"we've never taken a cooking course before. It just looked like fun."

Lillian called the class to take their seats then, and Carl and Helen chose two in the second row, against the windows. Helen took out a notepad and a slim blue pen.

"No need for me to take notes when Helen is here," Carl said quietly to the young woman, who had tentatively followed them to their seats. "My wife is the writer in the family."

HELEN HAD BEEN WRITING when Carl first met her, fifty years before, sitting in the central quadrangle of their college, surrounded by cherry trees dropping petals in great, snowy drifts. Actually, Carl always said when he told the story, Helen had not been writing, but thinking about it, chewing on her lip as if daring the words to make it past her teeth.

"Are you a writer, then?" he had said, sitting down on the concrete bench next to her, hoping that his opening line was a step beyond the horrifying "What's your major?" She gave him a long, considering look, during which time he decided he was getting no points for originality. The girl was a writer, after all, if being a writer meant watching the world from the cool remove of the mind. He swallowed and waited, unwilling to leave, yet determined not to make any further attempts at eloquence.

She clicked her pen shut and looked in his eyes. "Actually," she said, "I think I'd rather be a book."

And when he had nodded, as if hers was the most logical statement in the world, she smiled, and Carl realized he would be sitting in that moment for the rest of his life.

"WHAT'S ON FOR TONIGHT?" asked Claire from the front row of the class. Carl noticed that Claire was leaning forward eagerly; there was something different about her tonight—a haircut? Clothes? Helen would know, if he asked her, but Helen was focused on Lillian.

The counter Lillian stood behind was free of ingredients; a mixer, a rubber spatula, and several mixing bowls were all that the class could see reflected in the mirror that hung above the counter.

"So"—Lillian's eyes were playful—"I started you off with a pretty dramatic beginning last time, and you should be rewarded for being such good sports. Besides, fall is starting to make itself known and it seems like a good time for indulgence. Now, I want you all to tell me what you think about when I say cake."

"Chocolate."

"Frosting."

"Candles."

"Lamb cake," said Ian.

"Lamb cake?" asked Lillian, smiling. "What's that, Ian?"

Ian looked around the room and saw the others waiting,

intrigued. "Well, my dad always made it for Easter. White cake shaped like a lamb, with white icing and coconut shavings." He paused, then continued in a rush. "I hated coconut, and I thought the whole thing was stupid, but after I went away to college, all I could think about was how I wasn't going to get any of the lamb cake. And then about a week after Easter I got a padded envelope in the mail from my dad. Inside was this thing that looked like a frosted cow patty. I called my dad and you know what he said? 'Well, we missed you, son, so I sent you the lamb butt.' "

The other students laughed, and then the room quieted, waiting for the next story. The woman sitting next to Carl and his wife shifted slightly in her seat.

"Go on, Antonia," Lillian encouraged her, and the young woman spoke up, her accent thick and warm as sunshine.

"When I was growing up, in Italy, my family lived upstairs from a bakery. Every morning the smell of the bread baking would come up the stairs, under my door. When I came home from school, the glass cases would be full of little cakes, but they were always thin and flat, not so interesting. Sometimes, though, in the back, they would be making a big one, for a wedding." She sat back in her seat, smiling at the memory.

"I remember my wedding cake," said Claire. "I was so hungry—we hadn't eaten all day. Here was this incredible cake—layers of chocolate and whipped cream and all these curlicues of thick, smooth frosting—and they kept making us pose for pictures. I told my husband I was starving, and he took a fork and just stuck it in the side of the cake and fed me a bite. My mother and the photographer were furious, but I always tell James that was the moment when I married him."

Carl's and Helen's eyes met, sharing a silent joke.

"What was your wedding cake, Carl?" Lillian asked.

Carl smiled. "Ding Dongs."

The class turned in their seats to look at him.

"Well, Helen and I were on a budget—we didn't even go home to our parents to get married. We went to the courthouse after we finished spring finals, and spent our honeymoon in a little old hotel on the beach in northern California. The only store in town that was open was a gas station, and all they had were Ding Dongs—they called them Big Wheels back then—and shriveled old hot dogs."

"We took our Ding Dongs to the beach," Helen added, "and Carl found some sticks to use as pillars between them and he made a wedding cake tower. It was a thing of beauty."

"We kept the top one for our first anniversary, too, just like they tell you to," Carl finished, "didn't even have to freeze the thing." They laughed, along with the rest of the class.

"Well, then," said Lillian, "I think tonight we should make Carl and Helen a cake."

The class nodded hungrily.

"What flavor should it be?" Lillian asked Helen and Carl.

"White," said Helen decisively. "For our hair color." She took hold of Carl's hand and smiled.

. . .

HELEN HAD NOT BEEN available the cherry blossom day when Carl sat down next to her—and she wasn't available for a long time after. Carl didn't mind waiting, but he didn't intend it to be a passive experience. He chose the debate team, in which Helen was an avid member and which he saw as a better option than the campus book club or the women's soccer team, which took up the rest of Helen's free time. Helen's current boyfriend was on the debate team as well, and Carl found the prospect of a direct challenge to be more interesting.

In the end, he found he liked the debate team; he was a thorough and steadfast researcher, with arguments grounded in unassailable fact, and he had a passionate sense of righteousness that overcame any of his initial concerns about speaking in public and which not so much later caused him to contradict Helen in the midst of a mock debate. She stopped, stunned, and looked at him carefully. Then she grinned.

One evening in October, Carl walked into the Autumn Social Dance and saw Helen, standing on the side of the room talking with three of her friends. Her dark blue dress swirled out from her waist and clung at the bodice. Her hair fell to her shoulders in waves. The music began and Helen's friends were commandeered by their various beaus. Helen stood, watching them.

"Where's Mr. Debate Team?" Carl asked as he walked up.

"He's out of town. Leastways, he says he is." Helen contin-ued watching the dancers, her face steady.

"Care to practice some steps with me?" Carl asked, lightly. Helen considered him, a question asked and discarded in her eyes, then turned into the circle of his arms.

It stunned him how easy it was, after all that time wait-ing, to slip his right hand along her back and feel his fingers fit perfectly into the curve of her waist, to feel her fingers slide along the palm of his left hand and then rest softly in place. She followed his lead like water and his feet moved as if answer-ing instructions from a far better dancer. Without thinking, he pulled her closer to him and felt no resistance, only the slight incline of her forehead toward his shoulder. She was warm, and her hair smelled like cinnamon.

When the dance was over, he kept her close to him, her hand in his like a flower he had picked. She bent her head back slightly to look up at him.

"You're home," he said. She smiled and he leaned down to kiss her.

"IN MY OPINION, a cake is a lot like a marriage," Lillian began, as she brought eggs, milk, and butter from the refrigerator and put them on the counter. "Admittedly, I don't have a lot of experience," she remarked, holding up her ringless left hand with a wry expression on her face, "but I've often thought that it would be a great idea for couples to make their own wedding cakes, as part of the preparation for their life together. Maybe not so many couples would end up getting married"—Lillian smiled—"but I think those that did might approach it a bit differently."

She reached into the drawers below the counter and pulled out containers of flour and sugar and a box of baking soda.

"Now, cooking is all about preference—add a bit more of this or that until you reach the taste you want. Baking, however, is different. You need to make sure you have certain combinations correct."

Lillian took the eggs and separated the yolks from the whites into two small blue bowls.

"At its essence, a cake is actually a delicate chemical equation—a balance, between air and structure. You give your cake too much structure, and it becomes tough. Too much air and it literally falls apart.

"You can see why it would be tempting to use a mix"—her eyes sparkled—"but then you'd lose out on all the lessons that baking a cake has to teach you."

Lillian put the butter into the bowl and turned on the mixer; the paddles beat their way into the soft yellow rectangles. Slowly, in an impossibly thin waterfall of white, she let the sugar drift into the bowl.

"This is how you put air into a cake," she commented over the noise of the machine. "Back before mixers, it used to take a really long time. Every air bubble in the batter came from the energy of someone's arm. Now we just have to resist the urge to go faster and turn the mixer speed up. The batter won't like it if you do that." The waterfall of sugar ended, and Lillian stood, waiting patiently, watching the mixer.

The paddles continued their revolutions around the bowl, and the class watched the image in the mirror above the counter, entranced, as the sugar met and mingled with the butter, each drawing color and texture from the other, expanding, softening, lifting up the sides of the bowl in silken waves. Minutes passed, and still Lillian waited. Finally, when the butter and sugar reached the cloudlike consistency of whipped cream, she turned off the motor.

"There," she said. "Magic."

AFTER THEY WERE MARRIED, Carl and Helen decided to move to the Pacific Northwest. Helen had heard stories about tall trees and green that went on forever; she said she was ready for a change in color. Carl delighted in her sense of adventure and the idea of a new home for their new marriage. He got a job as an insurance agent—selling stability, he called it, giving his clients the luxury of sleeping through the night, knowing that no matter what happened there was a net into which they could fall, mid-dream.

The Pacific Northwest was dark and wet for much of the year, but Carl liked the mist that blanketed the trees and grass and houses. It was liquid fairy dust, he told his children when they arrived, two in quick succession starting in the third year of his and Helen's marriage. Their offspring were native north-westerners, raising their faces to the damp skies the way tulips follow the sun. Carl marveled at how the rain seemed to nour-ish them, watching as they sank their roots deep into the soil around them.

Helen found ways to sneak summer into the dark months of the year, canning and freezing the fruit off their trees in July and August and using it extravagantly throughout the winter—apple chutney with the Thanksgiving turkey, raspberry sauce across the top of a December pound cake, blueberries in Janu-ary pancakes. And she always claimed the shorter winter days with their long stretches of cool, gray light were conducive to writing. Carl had bought her a small wooden desk, which fit as if built for the nook at the top of the stairs. Helen always said, though, that she was a sprinter when it came to writing, com-posing in quick snatches at the kitchen table, in bed—although after the children arrived, the snatches of time occasionally were marathon distances apart.

Wherever she wrote, whatever she did, she was his Helen, and Carl loved her as completely in the silvery light of the Northwest as he had on the beach in northern California where they had honeymooned. Helen, in turn, filled his life, and just when he would least expect it in those first years, there in his lunch he would find a Ding Dong. On those days, he left work early.

. . .

LILLIAN PUT A FINGER into the bowl. "I always think this is the most delicious stage of a cake." She licked her finger with the enthusiasm of a child. "I'd give you some," she teased, "but then we wouldn't have enough for the cake."

Lillian took eggs out of the bowl of warm water. "So, now we add the egg yolks, bit by bit, letting the air rise into them as well." The mixer began its revolutions again as the liquid blended into the sugar-butter, the yolks turning the batter darker again, loose and glistening.

"After this," she noted, "no snacking on the batter. With raw eggs, it's too risky."

THE YEARS WHEN the children were small felt like a gift to Carl. He had come from a family that regarded affection with a kind of benign intellectual amusement, and the astonishing physical love of his children filled him with gratitude. Although he and Helen had, without speaking, fallen into the traditional roles of their generation—he left the house and earned the money, she took care of the home and children—Carl found himself breaking the rules whenever possible, waking at the baby's first noise and picking her up before Helen could rise. He sank into the warmth of his child's fragile body against his shoulder; watched in awe that a baby, still essentially asleep, could keep a death grip on the blanket that meant the world was safe and loving, marveling at the thought that it was he and Helen who gave the feeling to the blanket, and the blanket to the child.

He didn't even mind those early Christmas mornings when first one, then another toddler would climb into the bed that he and Helen had so recently fallen into themselves after a night of putting together wooden wagons, or bicycles, or dollhouses. He opened his arms and they piled in, trying to convince him that the streetlight outside really was the sun and that it was certainly time to open stockings, if maybe not presents, when in fact it was usually only two in the morning. Helen would groan good-naturedly and roll over, telling Carl all she wanted for Christmas was a good night's sleep, and he would pull the children close and whisper the story of the Night Before Christmas until they would slowly, one by one, fall asleep, their bodies draped across each other like laundry in the basket. When the children got older, self-sufficient enough to go on their own midnight exploratory missions among the boxes under the tree (where, more often than not, Carl and Helen discovered them sleeping in the morning), Carl found himself missing their warm intrusions into his dreams.

"Now it's time to add the flour." Lillian took the lid off the container. "The way I see it," she remarked, lifting out a scoopful and letting it fall through the sifter in a fluttering snow shower into the large measuring cup. "Flour is like the guy in the movie who you don't realize is sexy until the very end. I mean, be honest, when you are dividing up duties in the kitchen, who wants to be in charge of the flour? Butter is so much more alluring. But the thing is, flour is what holds a cake together."

Lillian began adding some of the flour to the batter, then milk.

"There is a trick, though," she commented, as she alternated adding flour and milk one more time, ending with a last portion of flour by hand. "If you mix the flour with the other ingredients for too long you will have a flat, hard cake. If you are careful, however, you'll have a cake as seductive as a whisper in your ear.

"And now, one last step," she said. Lillian beat the egg whites into a foam, adding just a bit of sugar at the end, as the class watched it turn into soft, then stiff peaks. When it was done, Lillian carefully folded the frothy cumulus clouds into the batter, a third at a time. She looked up and gazed out at the class. "Always save a bit of magic for the end."

CARL HAD BEEN forty-four when Helen had told him she had had an affair—over by that point, but she just couldn't keep it from him anymore, she had said. It was the most stunning thing that had ever happened to him, a rogue wave when he thought he understood the elements about him. Helen sat across from him at their kitchen table, crying, and he realized he had no idea whose life he had suddenly walked into. He remembered odd things at that moment—not the first time he had kissed Helen, but the time soon after, when he had walked up behind her as she was standing in her small dormitory kitchen and he touched his lips to the back of her neck.

She didn't want to leave him, she said, and she didn't want him to leave her. She loved him, always had; she just needed for him to know. He found himself wishing that she, who could keep a Christmas secret from their children for months without wavering, could have kept this one for herself—not forever, but for a while, as if in recognition that some announcements need anticipation to ease their transitions into our lives, a chance to feel the wavering doubts, to note the passenger seat of the car set to measurements not our own, the last cup of coffee taken from the pot without an offer to share.

It was, as Carl would later say, a spectacular failure of imagination on his part. He, who inhabited the future every day in his job, who helped people prepare for disaster of any magnitude, hadn't seen any signs. Helen insisted that was because she had never changed how she felt about him, but he couldn't believe that was strictly true. He wondered how he hadn't known and if he hadn't—as was so obviously the case—how he would ever know anything again. He lay in bed at night next to Helen, and thought.

Carl knew the statistics for divorce, of course. It was part of his job. In fact, statistics predicted a far greater chance of divorce than automobile accident, death by violence, or the all-too-graphic possibility of "dismemberment"—which was perhaps why insurance companies didn't sell policies for marital stability. In the weeks after his conversation with Helen, Carl found himself observing the young couples who came to his office, fascinated that people would spend hundreds of dollars a year insuring against the chance that someone might slip on their front steps in ice that rarely made an appearance in the coastal Northwest, yet go to bed each night uninsured against the possibility that their marriage might be stolen the next day. Perhaps, he thought, imagination fails when the possibilities are so obvious.

CARL SAID YEARS LATER that it was his very lack of imagination that had caused his marriage to continue. As easy as it was, after Helen told him, to imagine his wife with someone else— he knew, after all, which drink she would order if she wanted courage (scotch, straight up), which stories were her favorites to tell about the children (Mark and the bunny, Laurie learning how to swim), how she might touch the tip of her nose and dip her chin if she found one of his (the other his) jokes funny—as easy as it was to imagine all that, to realize how neatly all his knowledge of his wife could be spun out into a continually rolling film he had no desire to see, he could not imagine the next forty years without her.

What would he do with his long legs if he could no longer stretch them across the bed to warm her side while she brushed her teeth in the bathroom (thirty seconds each side, up and down, her toe tapping out the time)? Who would leave the kitchen cupboards open if she left, or catch the fragments of his sentences as they traveled across a dining room table littered with the unending commentary of their children? What would be the point of changing gears in their old we-ought-to-get-rid-of-it car, if not to touch her hand, which always rested on the gearshift as if (it was a family joke) to claim ownership?

He couldn't imagine, couldn't see, a failure of comprehension on the smallest, and thus largest, of levels. He waited for illumination and with it a direction that would lead him away from his home, his wife, but it didn't come. He tried to think forward, and simply couldn't. He and Helen lay, night after night, in bed, not touching, sat at the table and swapped plans for the day over coffee in the morning, told stories about the office or the children in the evening. And slowly, as he waited for illumination, what had happened each day—a fight with a daughter or son, the first crocuses in the garden, Helen's embarrassment over a haircut—began to pile up against what he could not imagine, until the secret she couldn't keep became one more part of their lives, one more stick in the nest they had built of moments and promises, the first time he had seen her, the second time they had fought, his hand touching her hair as she nursed a baby. Carl was a bird-watcher; he knew that not all sticks in a nest are straight.

. . .

CARL'S OLDER SISTER didn't understand. She had noticed some-thing was wrong and badgered him until he told her. Months later, at Thanksgiving, she found him in the kitchen as he was cleaning the carcass of the turkey after dinner.

"How long can you live like this?" she asked him.

"We made a promise, a long time ago." Carl's fingers moved among the bones of the turkey, pulling out the pieces of meat and stacking them on the plate beside him. Helen would be making them into sandwiches, turkey hash, and pot pie for the next two weeks, until the children would come down to the dinner table making gobbling noises, declaring they were the ghosts of turkeys past.

"She broke the promise, Carl." But her tone was gentle.

"We are keeping as much of it as we can." Carl looked down at the dog waiting patiently at his feet, and dropped a small piece of turkey to the floor. "Marriage is a leap of faith. You are each other's safety net."

"People change."

Carl stopped, and let his fingers rest on the counter in front of him. "I think that's what we're both counting on."

LILLIAN LIFTED the cake pans from the oven and rested them on metal racks on the counter. The layers rose level and smooth from the pans; the scent, tinged with vanilla, traveled across the room in soft, heavy waves, filling the space with whispers of other kitchens, other loves. The students found themselves leaning forward in their chairs to greet the smells and the memories that came with them. Breakfast cake baking on a snow day off from school, all the world on holiday. The sound of cookie sheets clanging against the metal oven racks. The bakery that was the reason to get up on cold, dark mornings; a croissant placed warm in a young woman's hand on her way to the job she never meant to have. Christmas, Valentine's, birthdays, flowing together, one cake after another, lit by eyes bright with love.

With a deft, quick motion, Lillian poked the golden surface of one of the layers with a toothpick and pulled it out, clean.

"Perfect," she said. "While it cools we can make the frosting."

Lillian paused, gathering her ideas.

"When we were making the body of the cake," she began, "everything was about keeping a balance between air and structure. Now we are putting the cake and the frosting together and it is the contrast that's important, that will make you take the second bite, and the one after.

"That's why an all-white cake is especially tricky. We can't get our contrast from flavor, not in any obvious way. We have no options for chocolate in our frosting, or raspberry preserve filling. No strawberries or lemon zest scattered across the top or hiding between the layers—although any of those could be fun another time.

"A white cake is the opposite of fireworks and fanfare—it's subtle, the difference in texture between the cake and the frosting as they cross your tongue. It's a little harder to accomplish"— she smiled at Helen and Carl—"but I have to say, when it works, it is sublime."

IT WAS A SATURDAY AFTERNOON, almost two years after Helen first told Carl about the affair. The kids were off preparing for Mark's high school graduation. Carl came up the basement stairs and heard a voice in French, with Helen's halting repetition afterward. He reached the door of the kitchen and looked in. Helen was standing with her back to him, a tape player balanced precariously on the window ledge, ingredients for a chocolate cake laid out on the counter around her. Helen had never been a particularly tidy cook, and the evidence was everywhere, flour dusting down to the floor, in wide streaks on her apron, melted chocolate dripping across the counter.

The tape stopped and Helen, deep in concentration, didn't notice. Cakes had always been an elusive prey for Helen. Diligently she had made them for every birthday and celebration— flat, misshapen, rock-hard, molten; Laurie still talked about what she called the volcano cake from her fifth birthday. And yet Carl knew Mark had begged for one; his graduation was that evening and it wouldn't be a celebration without a cake from Helen.

Carl stood at the door to the kitchen, not moving, watch-ing the late afternoon light filtering through the window and across Helen, coming to rest on the black and white tiles of the floor beneath her feet. He looked at the flour print on her hip where she had placed her hand while reading the next step in the recipe, at the white that was beginning to slip into her hair, strands that he loved and thus didn't tell her about, as he knew she would pull them out. He looked at her, without speaking, and as he looked, he felt something shift and come to rest inside him, a movement as small and quiet as the tick of a watch.

He walked up behind her and softly touched his lips to the back of her neck. Helen turned to face him, meeting his eyes for a long moment, as if measuring the weight of something within them. Then she smiled.

"You're home," she said, and reached up to kiss him.

THE CLASS STOOD companionably around the wooden counter, trying to navigate forkfuls of cake into their mouths without losing a crumb to the floor. The frosting was a thick butter-cream, rich as a satin dress laid against the firm, fragile texture of the cake. With each bite, the cake melted first, then the frost-ing, one after another, like lovers tumbling into bed.

"Oh, this is delicious!" Claire looked across the table to Carl and Helen. "I can't believe I made James choose chocolate for our wedding."

"Definitely beats lamb cake," Ian commented with a grin.

The fragile-looking older woman stood quietly, savoring the bite in her mouth. Lillian leaned over to her. "Penny for the memory, Isabelle," she said.

"Oh, my memories cost more than that these days—supply and demand, you know," Isabelle said with a chuckle, then continued. "I was thinking of Edward, my husband, when I was younger. He was so handsome on our wedding day, so solicitous. It didn't last—but it was nice remembering."

While the others continued talking, Carl and Helen stood next to each other, eating quietly. She was left-handed and he was right; as they ate, their free hands would find each other and let go, while their shoulders brushed against each other gently.

One piece of cake lay on the plate at the end of class; Lillian wrapped it in foil and handed it to Carl and Helen as they left the class.

"For you to take home," she said. "A symbol of a long and happy marriage."

"Or maybe . . ." Helen looked at Carl, who smiled and nodded. Helen took the foil package and went quickly out the door. Lillian and Carl watched as she caught up with Claire at the front gate. The two women talked for a few moments, then Helen leaned in and kissed Claire on the cheek. When Helen walked back to the kitchen, her face was radiant, her hands empty.

Antonia

Antonia drove up to the address written in her notebook and stopped, amazed. In a checkerboard neighborhood of craftsman bungalows and 1950s brick ramblers, the old Victorian house stood tall and splendid despite its obvious years of wear, the talcum-powder paint and tangled rhododendron bushes, the downspout hanging loose in the air like an arm caught in mid-wave. It was impossible to look at the house without erasing the years and the houses around it, to imagine it set in the midst of a vast track of land, gazing out across a long, rolling slope of green to the water and the mountains beyond. A home built by a man besotted, for a woman to whom he had promised the world.

Around the house, arched gateways led to a series of flower-beds and doll-size orchards, moss-covered stone benches, a circular lawn. Antonia knew the gardens had nothing to do with her work as a kitchen designer. All the same, she couldn't resist wandering through them, one after another like fairy stories in a well-loved children's book, even though it meant leaving her sodden shoes at the front door when she finally did enter the house.

The sound of the door closing behind her bounced off the tall ceilings of the entry hall and up the wide, wooden staircase leading to the second story. Her clients would not be the first people to change the house, she observed as she looked about her. Black and white linoleum tile made a chessboard of the front hallway; the parlor to her right was a startling shade of fuchsia. But in the living room to her left she could see the thin strips of the original oak floors and a trio of bay windows framing a group of ancient cherry trees, their knobby branches twisting toward the sky. She crossed the formal dining room, adrift without its table and chairs, and into the kitchen that was the reason for her visit.

It was a generous room, with yet another bay for a small eating table that seemed set into the garden itself, and space in the center of the room for a large, battle-scarred wooden prep table that claimed ownership with an air of long-standing occupation. But it appeared the former owners' remodeling urges had extended to the kitchen as well. Judging by the fake oak cabinets and the orange Formica countertop, the avocado and turquoise linoleum gracing the floor, Antonia guessed a 1970s burst of creativity. Still, cabinets could be changed and the spaces were good. Very good.

Antonia went over to the prep table, running her fingers affectionately along its worn surface, then looked beyond it to the other end of the kitchen, where a huge brick fireplace, blackened with age and use, was set in its own ten-foot-tall wall, flanked on one side by a mammoth six-burner stove and on the other by a window seat looking out to the raised beds of a deserted kitchen garden. Antonia walked to the fireplace and touched the soot gently with her fingers, bending her head to the opening and inhaling deeply, waiting for the smell of smoke and sausages, the sound of juices dripping and hissing on the hot wood below.

The front door opened and she heard the eager voices of her clients as they walked through the house.

"Antonia, are you already here?" Susan walked into the kitchen with a purposeful step. "There you are! Isn't the house marvelous?"

Antonia nodded and straightened up, wiping her hands surreptitiously on the back of her black pants before reaching out to shake hands with Susan and her husband-to-be.

"I mean, it's horrible." Susan laughed. "We're going to have to do everything over, of course. I mean, those cabinets and the floor—and that fireplace, for God's sake—but it will be worth it when we're done."

Antonia nodded. She always nodded at this stage; there really wasn't anything else to do.

"I'm thinking something minimal, industrial. Lots of stainless steel—I love stainless steel—with a concrete floor and black cabinets." Susan's hands gestured and pointed. "No handles—I hate handles—and maybe some rows of open metal shelves above the countertops. We could put the dishes and the new pots and pans up there." She turned to her fiancé, who smiled and nodded.

Antonia waited, thinking perhaps there would be more, but this appeared to be the end.

"So we'll just leave you to do your magic for a little while. Jeff and I need to go talk master bathroom, anyway. We're going to have to take out the whole third bedroom just to get a decent master suite!" And with another laugh, she was gone.

"It's a nice house," Jeff said to Antonia, before he left.

"Yes," she replied warmly. "It is."

Antonia stood in the kitchen, trying in her mind to lay the outline of Susan's vision over the kitchen that existed, but the straight lines kept bumping into the curve of the bay, sharp edges rumpled by the cushion on a window seat, the rounded back of an imaginary chair, warmed and softened by the fire-place that somehow, in every iteration, never seemed to give way to the image that Susan had presented.

In Antonia's four years in America, in her four years of designing kitchens in eighty-year-old cottages and colonial man-sions, contemporary condos and doll-size Tudors, this was the first fireplace she had seen in a kitchen, and she found herself circling it like a child with a dessert she knows is not for her. Antonia had grown up in a stone house, lived in by generations of families whose feet had worn dips into its limestone steps, where the smells of cooking had seeped into the walls like a marinade. It had taken her years to get used to the idea of houses made of wood, and she still found herself pacing the rooms of her rented bungalow when the wind was high and whistling. As she had watched how easily a wall could be taken down to open up a kitchen to a family or dining room, however, she had come to appreciate a certain invitation to creativity inherent in wooden structures; it offset a bit her feeling that nothing she worked on was likely to last.

But here was a fireplace. It reminded Antonia of her grand-mother's kitchen, with its stove at one end and a hearth at the other, the space in the middle long and wide enough to accom-modate a wooden table for twelve and couches along the sides of the room. Her grandmother's cooking area was small—a tiny sink, no dishwasher, a bit of a counter—but out of it came tortel-lini filled with meat and nutmeg and covered in butter and sage, soft pillows of gnocchi, roasted chickens that sent the smell of lemon and rosemary slipping through the back roads of the small town, bread that gave a visiting grandchild a reason to run to the kitchen on cold mornings and nestle next to the fire-place, a hunk of warm, newly baked breakfast in each hand. How many times had she sat by the fire as a little girl and listened to the sounds of the women at the other end of the kitchen, the rhythmic rap of their knives against the wooden cutting boards, the clatter of spoons in thick ceramic bowls, and always their voices, loving, arguing, exclaiming aloud in laugh-ter or mock horror at some bit of village news. Over the course of the day, the heat from the fireplace would stretch across the kitchen toward the warmth of the stove until the room filled with the smells of wood smoke and meat that had simmered for hours. Even as a little girl, Antonia knew that when the two sides of the kitchen met, it was time for dinner.

Standing in Susan and Jeff's kitchen, Antonia felt her stomach tighten with homesickness. She hadn't realized how strong the feeling was, how much she longed for everything this fireplace, this well-worn wooden table meant to her—a life of language rolling off the tongue like a caress, of houses that nourished the heart as well as the eye.

"Is it going to work?" Susan asked, returning to the kitchen, her face lit with plans. "I mean, I know it's small, but if we do it right, there will be room for both of us to cook, and . . ."

Jeff looked at Antonia ruefully. "Which means, I suppose, we'd have to learn?"

"Of course," Susan exclaimed. "I got some great cookbooks at our wedding shower!"

Antonia smiled politely. "I'll work up some sketches. Shall we meet here again, say in a week or so?"

"That would be fabulous." Susan was opening cupboards, and turned with a laugh. "Really, this is just awful. I'm so glad you can see what we are looking for."

"I DON'T KNOW how to do this," Antonia told her boss in misery.

"What's the problem?" he asked.

"She doesn't want a place to cook. She wants a kitchen for people to see her in."

"You've dealt with those kind of clients before—more than once, and you've done beautifully."

"But this kitchen—you'd have to see it. I can't take it apart."

"But it's not your kitchen, Antonia, and they are the clients. You'll have to see through their eyes. Or," he added teasingly, "figure out a way to make them see through yours."

WHEN ANTONIA HEARD Lillian announce that that night's cooking class was to prepare a Thanksgiving dinner, she shuddered. It had been a long weekend; she was no closer to having a design for Susan and Jeff's kitchen than she had been when she first walked into their house, and she had been hoping to avoid Thanksgiving this year. She had been invited, every year of her four in the United States, to one Thanksgiving fest or another. Americans seemed to love sharing their cultural traditions, as if they were shiny new cars or babies. Every year Antonia sat at a table awash with food, watching serving bowls the size of laundry baskets being passed from one end to the other, dollops of mashed potatoes and creamed onions and cranberry sauce and bread stuffing and whipped yams and hunks of turkey plopping down, one after another, onto a plate already full. The point seemed to be to eat as much as possible before falling asleep. It made a certain sense for a holiday celebrating survival over starvation, and everyone seemed to revel in the excess of it all, but she couldn't help feeling embarrassed for the food, all smashed together like immigrants in steerage class. She knew, sitting in Lillian's kitchen, that her face had shown her thoughts and she quickly suppressed them.

"Actually, we're going to try something a little different tonight," Lillian said, smiling at Antonia. "I believe in traditions— they hold us together, like bones—but it can be easy to forget what they are really about. Sometimes we need to look from a different perspective to find them again."

Lillian focused her attention on their faces. "So—what is the essence of Thanksgiving?"

"It's about coming together," said Helen warmly. "All these different people, with all their different lives, being a family."

"Or at my house," Chloe spoke up, a pinch of bitterness in her words, "it's about everyone being the same, and if you're not, eating enough so you won't notice." Chloe glanced around at the other students. "Sorry, Helen."

"Well," Lillian suggested, "here's an idea: Instead of thinking about the people, how about we approach the food we will be preparing like the guest list for a dinner party—each dish invited for its own personality, all of them playing off one another to make the meal more interesting.

"And you never know," she added, "if you treat the food that way, perhaps the people will follow." Lillian started passing out a stack of menus written on thick white paper. "I'm going to try this at the restaurant this year. I thought it would be fun to do a dry run with the class."

Antonia looked down at the paper that was passed to her and read:

THANKSGIVING DINNER

Pumpkin ravioli

Stuffed turkey breast with rosemary,
cranberries, and pancetta

Polenta with Gorgonzola

Green beans with lemon and pine nuts

Espresso with chocolate biscotti

"It's different, I agree," Lillian noted, "but in the end, you'll see that almost all the traditional Thanksgiving ingredients are there—even the original Indian corn—it's just not the way you might expect. We'll see what it makes you think about Thanksgiving.

"Now, this is a lot to do, so we'll divide into teams and you can compare notes over dinner. I actually will give you recipes this time—although somehow I think you'll still find the recipes a little atypical." Lillian's eyes were laughing. "Ian and Helen, I'd like you to work on the ravioli; Antonia and

Isabelle, you're on turkey; Carl and Tom, I'll let you take over the polenta; and Claire and Chloe, you're in charge of the biscotti. I've got your recipes and the ingredients laid out at different stations, and I'm here if you have questions."

With that, Lillian opened the oven and took out a roasted wedge of pumpkin, its juices sputtering in the bottom of the pan.

"And one more thing," Lillian added, "we'll be eating slowly tonight—one course at a time, as they are ready. Every guest at a table should feel appreciated."

ANTONIA AND ISABELLE stood at their prep area, Isabelle's silver hair and pale blue eyes making Antonia's dark hair and olive skin seem even more vibrant. In front of them on the counter lay a mound of glistening turkey breast, deep green spikes of rosemary, creamy-white garlic cloves, wrinkled dried cranberries, slices of pink and white pancetta, salt, pepper, olive oil.

"You know," Isabelle commented by way of introduction, "before you start cooking with me, I should tell you, I am losing my way, these days."

Antonia's hands stopped their movement among the ingredients. She looked at Isabelle quietly. "You are lost?" she said gently.

"No," replied Isabelle. "I'm just not always sure where I am. Memories hold you to the ground, you know? And I"—she touched the dried cranberries with the tip of her finger—"am a bit light on my feet these days."

Antonia picked up a sprig of rosemary and raised it to Isabelle's nose. "Breathe in," she suggested.

Isabelle inhaled and her face opened like a morning glory. "Greece." The word came out with a sigh. "My honeymoon. There were rosemary hedges leading to our little stone house. The gardener came and clipped them one morning, and we made love in that green air for hours." Isabelle stopped, embarrassed, and looked at Antonia.

"That's lovely," Antonia said.

"But maybe you should hold the knife, my dear," Isabelle responded. She picked up the paper Lillian had given them and laughed. "Now, this would be Lillian's idea of a recipe."

On the paper was written: "Take ingredients on the prep table, chop as need be. Butterfly turkey and flavor inside and out, as you like. Make a package. Send it."

"We can work with that," Antonia said.

She chopped the herbs and garlic, the sharp knife making swift, delicate cuts, filling the air around them with the scent of forests and earth and hot sun. Isabelle laid the turkey breast out like a butterfly with its wings spread, and Antonia slid the knife into the meat, starting from the center, cutting parallel to the cutting board, slicing each section so they lay open half again as thin, a series of butterflies. Across the blank canvas of turkey, Isabelle sprinkled salt and pepper, then delicate pieces of garlic and rosemary. The two women looked at the cranberries.

"You know . . ." Isabelle started.

"They need something," Antonia agreed.

"Sherry?"

"Lillian said we are playing with tradition, yes?"

They took a bottle from the cooking cabinet and poured some in a small dish, adding the dried cranberries after. The women watched as the berries grew larger and softer as they absorbed the liquid.

"We'll just let that sit for a while," said Isabelle, dipping a finger into the mixture and tasting it.

"Dinner parties," she said, "with little glasses of sherry beforehand. My husband brought his secretary."

"I'm sorry." Antonia touched Isabelle's wrist.

"It's a pity you have no say in which memories you lose," Isabelle remarked. "There was this sculptor, later, but I can't always find him in my head now . . ."

"Wait here, just a minute." Antonia walked across the kitchen to where Ian and Helen were working on the pasta for the ravioli. "Would you mind if I borrowed just a bit of that?" she asked, pointing to the mound of dough, soft and dusty with flour.

Ian looked at her confused, but Helen only smiled.

"Of course, dear. All you need."

Antonia carried her prize back to Isabelle, where she pressed the dough gently on the counter into a smooth, flat oval. "Here," she said, taking Isabelle's fingers and gliding them over the sur-face of the pasta, "maybe this will help you remember."

Isabelle's eyes lit brilliantly blue. "Thank you," she said, and grew quiet for a moment.

They drained the red-tinged sherry from the cranberries, tasting as they went. Isabelle dropped the swollen berries like a long ruby necklace across the rosemary and garlic, Antonia adding a thin stream of milky-green olive oil, finally covering the mixture with slices of translucent pink and white pancetta. Together they rolled the turkey up with the tips of their fingers, adding an extra layer of seasoning and pancetta on the outside. When they were done, Antonia held the meat in place while Isabelle tied a white cotton string around it.

"Blame it on the sherry," Isabelle commented, looking at her work. They wrapped the turkey in foil, and it did indeed look like a present, which they put in the oven.

"Congratulations," Lillian said, handing them each a glass of sparkling Prosecco. "Now that you are done with knives, you can have a glass of this. The pasta is almost ready. Come help with the dining room."

LILLIAN HAD TAKEN several of the smaller square tables and made a long rectangular one, running along the center of the restaurant dining room, the tablecloth over it a starched white snowfield. Isabelle folded napkins of the same heavy material into sharply creased triangles and set them to mark each place, then fetched silverware and white dinner plates. With a taper,

Antonia lit the candles that ran down the length of the table, their yellow glow reflecting in the thick, uneven glass of the old windows.

The rest of the class came in from the kitchen, led by a triumphant Ian and Helen, carrying a large steaming platter. Ian held the serving dish while Helen carefully placed on each white plate five squares of ravioli no thicker than paper, their edges crinkled, their surfaces kissed with melted butter, scattered with bits of shallots and hazelnuts, like rice thrown at a wedding.

They each took their places at the table. "Happy Thanksgiving, everyone," Lillian said, raising her glass.

They sat for a moment, simply looking. The smell from their plates rose with the last bits of steam, butter releasing whispers of shallots and hazelnuts. Antonia raised a bite to her mouth. A quick crunch of hazelnut, and then the pasta gave way easily to her teeth, the pumpkin melting across her tongue, warm and dense, with soft, spicy undercurrents of nutmeg. It felt like going home, and she relaxed into her chair with a sigh of happiness. She looked about the table, wondering what the other students thought, watching as they ate slowly, and then more slowly, concentrating only on the flavors within their mouths, oblivious to the table around them. Ian's eyes caught hers.

"Do you like it?" she asked him. "The ravioli?"

"It is beyond good," he answered, enraptured. "I can't believe Helen and I made this."

"Hey, now," Helen interjected with a laugh from two seats down.

"You know what I mean," Ian responded. He paused, and then looked back at Antonia. "Do you eat like this all the time?"

"No . . ." she replied hesitantly.

"You do, don't you?" he replied quickly, "or at least you have. I mean, that explains a lot."

"What?"

"Why you . . ." Ian backtracked: "Never mind."

"He is saying you are beautiful," Isabelle said matter-of-factly, and put another bite in her mouth.

"Ahh . . ." Antonia looked down, a small smile on her face.

THE TURKEY EMERGED from the oven, juices sizzling within the metal wrapping.

"Here," said Antonia to Isabelle, "lean over the top." She opened the creased foil and Isabelle inhaled as the steam caressed her face.

"Christmas," Isabelle said. "My grandmother always cooked the entire dinner with things she had grown herself—except for the turkey; she got that from the neighbor. I loved to walk in her garden after dinner; it felt alive, even in the winter. She always told me that rosemary grows in the garden of a strong woman. Hers were like trees."

They left the turkey to finish cooking itself outside the oven and went to watch the others. Chloe and Claire were talking happily, enveloped in the comforting smell of chocolate. They had taken what looked like a long, thin layer of shiny cake from the oven and were cutting it into slices, turning them on their sides on the cookie sheet, where, like magic, they suddenly transformed into traditional oval biscotti.

Nearby, Carl and Tom were consulting over the pot of polenta as it bubbled and shot small bullets of hot, liquid corn into the air. Antonia noticed that for the moment Tom's expression had lost the sadness that clung to him like a signature.

"It's too hot!" Carl said.

"Let's turn it down, and then I think it's time to add the Gorgonzola," Tom suggested, picking up crumbles of milky cheese, blue-veined like marble.

Antonia peeked over their shoulders. The polenta was a cauldron of summer, vibrantly gold against the black of the pot. Carl was stirring with a long-handled wooden spoon with a hole in the center while Tom dropped in small bits of cheese that left white comet trails as they melted into the moving yellow mass. Nearby, Lillian was squeezing a lemon over a mountain of green beans steaming in a white bowl.

"Antonia," she said, "can you take care of the pine nuts?"

Antonia took the long handle of the frying pan on the stove, gave it a quick shake to flip the pine nuts that were browning in the heat. A couple more flicks of her wrist and they were done, and she shook them across the top of the green beans like confetti tossed at the stroke of a new year. She looked up to find Tom watching her, his expression filled with sadness again. She gave him a questioning look.

"It's nothing," he said, shaking his head gently. "For a moment there, you reminded me of someone."

"Is that bad?" Antonia asked, concerned.

"No," said Tom, his face clearing. "It's a good thing."

"Are we ready?" asked Lillian, holding open the door to the dining room. They entered like a parade, bowls and platters held aloft.

"How do you like our dinner guests?" Lillian asked the class after the first exclamations had succumbed to quiet sighs of pleasure. The pace was leisurely, as each person at the table took slow, contemplative bites. The turkey lay in slices on their plates, palest pink, with spirals of herb and pancetta ribbons running through it. The polenta was a bright dash of color, the crisp tang of the green beans and lemon a contrast in taste to the soft, luxuriant texture of the warm cornmeal.

"This isn't eating," said Ian. "It needs its own word."

They had agreed that no one would pour their own wine, so they took turns walking around the table, filling glasses, stopping for a low-voiced moment of conversation with one person or another. Even Chloe was given some wine, although she wasn't yet twenty-one.

"I don't know, Chloe," Ian joked, "we could get in a lot of trouble because of you."

Isabelle leaned over the table to Chloe. "When I was young, we didn't worry about such things. But then again," she said with a wink, "maybe that is why I don't remember so much now."

They would have forgotten about the biscotti, except that Chloe was so proud of them she dragged Lillian off to the kitchen to make espresso, brought to the table in tiny white cups, a crisp oval of chocolate biscotto on the plate underneath.

"Now *that* was a wonderful Thanksgiving," Carl said, leaning back luxuriantly in his chair as he put down his empty espresso cup.

"You know, I always think a holiday is a lot like a kitchen," Lillian noted. "What's important is what comes out of it."

Antonia thought for a moment, then smiled. "But of course," she said quietly to herself.

It WAS well past eleven when they left the restaurant—the wine, the food, the conversations of the evening warming them even as they entered the cold, dark air.

"She didn't ask us what we learned about Thanksgiving," Ian commented.

"Did you want her to?" Helen asked.

Chloe tucked her arm companionably through Ian's.

"I bet you really liked to take tests in school," she teased him.

"I just want to know if I have to wait until Thanksgiving to eat like that again. Or if I don't, will Thanksgiving still be special?"

Antonia came up to him on his other side.

"No. And yes." Her eyes met his briefly, happily. They all reached the gate and Antonia turned and walked to the left, toward her car.

"*Buona notte, Antonia,*" Isabelle called into the night.

"*Sogni d'oro,*" sweet dreams, came Antonia's voice in reply.

ANTONIA HEARD Susan and Jeff on the porch before they entered the house.

"I can't wait to see the plans," Susan was saying as she opened the door. "She . . . Oh, my God, what is that incredible smell?"

Susan and Jeff reached the kitchen and stopped, wordless. The linoleum in the room in front of them had been ripped up, revealing a fir floor underneath, splotched with glue, but a warm red-gold all the same. A small table covered with a yellow Provençal tablecloth was set like a secret in the bay window; an iron pot full of water boiled cheerfully on the huge black stove. In the center of the room the wooden prep table was covered with a snowstorm of flour and a series of red ceramic bowls, and in the fireplace, on a grill set over a glowing bed of fragrant sticks, marinated chicken and eggplant sizzled and cooked.

"You're just in time," Antonia said. "Throw on an apron and you can help me finish the ravioli."

SUSAN WIPED the last of the meat juices from her plate with a piece of bread. Her normally sleek blond hair curled about her face in the humidity of the kitchen. Flour smudged the side of her black skirt and she had utterly forgotten to take off her apron when she sat down at the table.

"That was amazing," she moaned. Jeff looked at her and smiled, reaching across the table for her hand.

"Will you cook like this for us, always?" Susan asked Antonia.

"I think you will cook for each other, in this kitchen."

"Yes," Jeff agreed.

"Okay," Susan responded amiably. She took a leisurely, reflec-tive sip of her red wine. "We *can* change the cabinets, though, right? Please? Oh, wait—oh, this would be great—do you think we could find a photograph of the original kitchen, and see what the old ones used to look like?"

Jeff raised his wineglass to Susan. "That's my girl," he said.

. . .

ANTONIA ENTERED her wooden bungalow, took off her coat, and dialed the phone.

"It worked," she said happily into the receiver. "Thank you for helping me—how did you say, rip up?—the floor. I didn't know who else to call."

"Anytime," replied Ian.

Tom

Tom stood outside the restaurant kitchen. The windows were lit; he could see the other students inside, mingling with the easy familiarity of neighbors at a block party. On the counter, cans of tomatoes, a canister of flour, a paper-wrapped package, sat ready for the night's lesson. It was like coming home after a long day away, opening a door to the certainty that someone was there, had always been there. He turned to go.

"Hi, Tom." Lillian opened the kitchen door. Her dark hair was pulled back from her face, her eyes calm, watching him. She smiled.

"Come in," she said. "You'll get cold out there."

Something about Lillian's voice touched everyone who

heard it; it left you feeling protected, forgiven for things you hadn't even figured out you had done. When Lillian told you to enter a room, you did, if only to be near her voice.

"I thought it felt like a pasta night," Lillian remarked as Tom came into the kitchen. "Let's see if you agree with me."

THE STUDENTS FOUND their usual places in the rows of chairs facing the wooden counter. "It's chilly out there," Lillian addressed the class. "I hope you all are warming up." Her eyes ran over the rows of students, checking facial expressions, a jittery knee.

Tom followed her gaze. Claire was putting away her wallet; she had been showing photographs to Isabelle and a smile lingered on her face. Chloe had moved to the back row; her face was distracted, without the openness that had been there at the end of the Thanksgiving class. Tom noticed that Ian had finally secured a seat next to Antonia, although it appeared that he was still having a hard time figuring out what to say to her. Carl sat next to his wife, as always. She was resting her hand on his arm, the tip of her index finger just touching his wrist bone. Tom looked back to the front of the class.

"You know," Lillian began, "something always happens to me when the weather changes in the fall. Everything seems to be moving so quickly toward the cold. So this evening, I thought we would work with one of the most essential ingredients of all—time.

"Not the herb," she said, smiling at the look of confusion on Isabelle's face. "Minutes, hours. If you stop to think about it, every meal you eat, you eat time—the weeks it takes to ripen a tomato, the years to grow a fig tree. And every meal you cook is time out of your day—but you all know that.

"Now, usually a class about time is really about efficiency—how to do twice as much in half the time. But we are going to do exactly the opposite tonight. We are going to cultivate inefficiency, squander our best resource as if our supply was infinite. We are going to make a meal that flies in the face of the fact that every day is getting shorter for the next three months—pasta with red sauce.

"Now, to truly have this experience, you would need to begin in the morning, so the sauce could cook all day. Unfortunately, we don't quite have that amount of time, but you'll be able to learn the lesson anyway."

She picked up a head of garlic in her hand, as if weighing it, and then looked out across the class.

"Tom," she said, "why don't you come help me?" and she gently tossed the garlic. It landed in the bowl created by his palms, its outer layers crackling like a secret, the weight both heavier and lighter than he had anticipated. He didn't want this, not tonight when the world seemed both too cold and too warm. But the garlic lay in his hands, waiting. He gripped it,

hard, then stood and walked a bit uncertainly around the counter to Lillian's side, his cupped hands coming up to his face in
a gesture so automatic that he was surprised when the smell of
the garlic slipped into his nose.

CHARLIE HAD LOVED GARLIC; she had told Tom that if he loved
her, he'd better love the way her fingers smelled after a day in
the kitchen, the scent soaked deep into her skin like wine into
a tablecloth. She refused the aid of all kitchen gadgets, crush-
ing the fat, firm cloves under her strong thumb, pulling off the
papery outer sheets and digging her nail into the base of the
clove to remove the hardened end. She would have chopped
with her fingers, too, if she could have, burrowing into the
smell of it. When she was done, she would trace lines with her
fingertips between her breasts, along the base of her skull and
up behind her ears.

"Trails for you to follow," she would say to Tom with a
wink.

One evening at a restaurant, the wife of one of Tom's law
firm clients had commented despairingly on the amount of garlic on her bruschetta.

"Andy will never sleep with me tonight," she had remarked
with an embarrassed laugh. "Darling, did you bring mints
with you?"

While the couple was engaged in checking pockets and

purses, Charlie had met Tom's eyes across the table. Slowly, she ran her index finger over the thick, aromatic oil that had seeped into the toasted circles of bread on her plate. Then her hand disappeared under the table.

THE GARLIC LAY on the chopping board, cut into small, precise pieces. Lillian took the knife from Tom and pushed the pile into a small mound on the side of the board. Tom was surprised to see a pile of freshly cut onions next to it, their smell sharper, lightning instead of thunder.

"I thought I'd keep you company," Lillian commented. Grasping a half-gallon bottle of olive oil from under the counter, she hefted it up and poured a spiraling circle of thick, green-gold liquid into the large skillet on the stove. She turned the burner on with a small whoosh of air.

"Sometimes," she remarked, "the best meal requires you to forget that time exists. But then there's olive oil—olives start to change flavor within hours of when they are picked. After all those months of growing. That's why the best oil comes from the first press, and the very best is made close to its own trees."

TOM HAD MET CHARLIE eight years before, when they were both working the summer shift at a restaurant on Cape Cod.

Not that it was really a restaurant, or that he was really a cook, or that Charlie should have ever been a waitress, given her general attitude toward submissiveness. Considering Charlie's skills in the kitchen, it should have all been the other way around. But that was the way things worked at Lonny's.

Tom's first day he had been on the breakfast shift, turning over bacon with a long-handled spatula and trying to work up the courage to flip the frying egg that would soon no longer be over-easy. A woman with golden skin and sun-blond hair, an appearance rendered only slightly less stunning by the irony of her red-and-white-striped waitress outfit, walked up to him and grasped the handle of the frying pan. With one quick jerk forward and back she sent the egg up and over.

"Wish I could do that to table number seven," she remarked dryly, and headed back out of the kitchen.

She had found him again on his break. She handed him a frying pan, complete with a half-cooked egg.

"I'm Charlie," she said. "Flip this ten times for me." After his third failed attempt, she had grinned, taken the pan and shown him again, and he had fallen in love with the faint line of muscle that ran down her arm.

Tom quickly learned that Charlie couldn't keep her hands off food. She could mince an entire onion, left unprotected on the counter, before the prep cook could come back out of the walk-in refrigerator. The cooks were always yelling at her for sticking her fingers in the sauces. She would placate them flirta-

tiously, giving a seductive pause before hip-checking the swinging doors into the dining room. She often came by Tom's station
on her next pass through.

"Add a little nutmeg to the white sauce," she would com-
ment in a voice too low for anyone else to hear.

She called it guerrilla cooking. Tom knew that when he
wasn't there she simply added the ingredients herself, but he
liked that when he was there, she told him. He thought about
her at night, wondering what she would do to a pancake, a
pizza, the small surprises she would add to the lives of the people who sat at her tables.

She would eat anything. The nights they worked the closing shift, dancing on the trash in the bin until there was enough
room to add the last boxes and cans, they would finish and look
about them at the scrubbed-down kitchen. Then they would
grab the pans, the oils, the food Charlie had stashed at the back
of the walk-in, and start cooking for real. Salsa packed with
onions and cilantro, fresh white fish with garlic and soy and
tangerine juice. Many of the ingredients she brought herself—
the patrons of the restaurant would no more recognize tofu than
their own backsides, she was fond of saying. That Tom had
never seen tofu before either didn't concern Charlie.

"You're different," she would say. "Have a bite, and learn."

They would eat in the kitchen, shunning the dining room
with its paper napkins and plastic-coated red-and-white-checked
tablecloths. While they ate, she would recite the old English

poetry she refused to study anymore. Tom would tell her about the law courses he was taking, and she would listen, playing with the intricacies of the cases the way she would ingredients in a dish.

"What if . . . ?" she was always asking, and Tom would realize that her ideas, if applied to the legal system, would be as elegant and disturbing as fish roe and seaweed in a hamburger joint.

The first time he had kissed her—it had taken six weeks— was over hamburgers, two inches thick, juices running. He had leaned over and licked the grease off her arm without thinking. As he brought his face up to hers, he wondered how it was that the distance between arm and mouth could take such a sweet infinity to travel.

THE OIL COVERED the bottom of the pan, smooth and thick, the smallest of bubbles rising toward the surface.

"Now, we're going to take one of these," Lillian said to the class, holding up a flat square shape, covered in foil. "Does anyone know what it is?"

"*Dadi*," Antonia said in a delighted tone.

"They are more interesting than salt," Lillian said, "a little like a bouillon cube, but this type is a bit different." She opened the foil-wrapped package and placed the square, golden-brown shape in Tom's hand.

It was soft, almost greasy, unlike the hard bouillon cubes that had flavored the soups of Tom's childhood; this one crushed easily, leaving oil clinging to the ridges of his fingertips as he dropped the bits into the pan. Lillian stirred with a wooden spoon and the oil changed in texture, like liquid sand.

"Time for the onions," Lillian directed. Tom picked up the slippery pieces and dropped them in carefully. The smell rose toward his face; he started to pull back, then leaned in and breathed—bread and vineyards, warm in the sun.

Lillian put the wooden spoon in his hand and motioned toward the pan. He watched the moving pieces as they started to turn from white to clear, their hard shapes melting. Tom stirred, waiting for direction from Lillian as the onions began to drink in the liquid around them, almost disappearing into the color of the oil. Lillian leaned forward and added the garlic, but still she said nothing. Finally, as the garlic softened, but before the edges began to curl, Tom reached forward and took the pan off the burner.

"Perfect," she said quietly. The class let out a small collective sigh.

"Now we'll add the meat. You can try different varieties," she said, facing out toward the class, "depending on your mood. We'll use sausage this time." Waves of fennel and pepper, the smell of sizzling red meat, mingled with the air.

"Breathe in," Lillian said. "The air is different now. If you want a dish that is lighter, you can make this sauce with eggplant instead of meat. Or a summer version, with just olive oil and garlic and fresh tomatoes and fresh basil, cooked for a moment or two. But sometimes, especially in fall and winter, it's nice to have a little more intensity."

BEFORE TOM KISSED CHARLIE, he had felt as if she was in his every thought. Afterward, he knew differently. It was almost mortifying how the thought of making love to Charlie took over his most mundane meditations. He started taking a toothbrush to work, although he knew full well that she had no particular passion for the taste of plaque-reducing mint.

"Good God, man, have you given up law for dentistry?" she had asked.

But he couldn't help it. His lips, having touched Charlie's arm and mouth, wanted to wander, and where lips couldn't go, the mind would. Fried eggs, forgotten in the skillet, solidified into doorknobs, while Tom threw fries on the grill, lobbed steaks into the deep-fat fryer.

"Charlie, for Christ's sake," the dishwasher had yelled across the kitchen in exasperation, "would you give him a break before this whole place goes up in flames?"

Charlie walked back to Tom's station. She looked at the mess on the grill.

"Dinner, my house. Tonight," she said, then crossed the kitchen to the back door and punched out her time card. The prep cooks howled.

CHARLIE LIVED in a blue and orange cottage two houses away from the ocean. The paint had given up most of its color to the wind and sun years before; daisies and gladiolas grew with haphazard abundance, scattering petals across the gravel pathway that led to the house. When Tom arrived the front door was open, and he could see the inside of the cottage was tiny, with a futon that did daytime duty as the living room couch, and a kitchen large enough for a single slim cook.

Charlie stood at the stove, the wooden spoon in her hand. He could smell wine in the air, butter, and garlic.

"I just knew you'd be on time," she said. The skin below her ear was warm against his lips. She smiled, and nodded toward the counter, where he saw a blue bowl overflowing with chopped melon and a set of brilliant white plates. "You can take those out to the patio."

Tom ducked his head as he went out the back door and found himself under a trellis heavy with green vines and deep purple blossoms, the evening sunlight filtering down through the leaves. Beneath his feet was a patio made from old bricks that moved with his weight, clinking softly as he walked to the green metal table and placed the bowl and plates next to a

basket of bread. He stood straight again, his head almost touching the leaves, and breathed in the pepper-sweet smell of wisteria. Everything suddenly seemed twice as quiet as he thought it
ever could be.

"Wine?" asked Charlie, coming up behind him and handing him a glass. The wine was cold and clear and tasted like
flowers and snow. "I love this patio. It's why I rented the house,
really."

She returned to the kitchen and came back with a plate covered with slices of meat, thin as leaves.

"Prosciutto," she explained to his questioning eyes. "With
the melon. You'll see."

They sat at the tiny table, their toes touching as Charlie
ladled a spoonful of dripping melon chunks onto his plate.

"Taste the melon first," she suggested. "There's a guy at
the fruit stand who saves his best for me." She laughed when
she saw the expression on Tom's face. "He is very, very old.
And he loves his melons like children. You're lucky—this is
the time of year when they are at their best. And Angelo's
melons . . . well . . ."

Tom skewered a piece with his fork and put it in his mouth.
The flavor opened like a flower across his tongue, soft and
sweet. He started to talk, and then stopped, holding the taste
inside as it dissolved into juice.

Charlie watched him. "Now we'll try some prosciutto with
it." She took a piece of melon in her fingers, wrapped it with

a translucent slice of pink meat, and motioned for him to open his mouth. The meat was a whisper of salt against the dense, sweet fruit. It felt like summer in a hot land, the smooth skin in the curve between Charlie's strong thumb and index finger. The wine afterward was crisp, like coming up to the surface of water to breathe. They ate slowly, and yet more slowly, until the bowl was empty.

"Give me a minute," Charlie said. She stood, resting her hand for a moment on Tom's shoulder as she moved toward the kitchen. "I'll be back." Tom sat, listening to the sounds of Charlie moving about in the house—the clatter of a pot lid being set in the sink, a refrigerator being opened, shells rattling into a pan. Music drifted from the living room, a woman he had never heard before, in a language he didn't know. Charlie hummed along with the music; through the open back door Tom could catch sight of a hand, the back of her heel, as she moved from sink to stove. He remembered, as if from a long way away, a time when the world was huge; now it seemed as if he could fit all the world into such a small space—a restaurant, a house, a table, the hem of Charlie's skirt as it brushed against her ankle.

"*Spaghetti del mare,*" she said, coming through the door, "from the sea."

In the large, wide, blue bowl, swirls of thin noodles wove their way between dark black shells and bits of red tomato.

"Breathe first," Charlie told him, "eyes closed." The steam rose off the pasta like ocean turned into air.

"Clams, mussels," Tom said, "garlic, of course, and tomatoes. Red pepper flakes. Butter, wine, oil."

"One more," she coaxed.

He leaned in—smelled hillsides in the sun, hot ground,
stone walls. "Oregano," he said, opening his eyes. Charlie
smiled and handed him a forkful of pasta. After the sweetness
of the melon, the flavor was full of red bursts and spikes of hot
pepper shooting across his tongue; underneath, like a steadying
hand, a salty cushion of clam, the soft velvet of oregano, and
pasta warm as beach sand.

They ate. Bite after bite, plateful after plateful. They talked
about childhoods—Charlie was from the West Coast, Tom
from the East; Charlie had broken three bones in a bicycle fall,
Tom his nose when his older brother was learning to pitch
baseball. When the bowl was empty, they ran hunks of bread
along the sauce at the bottom and brought them dripping to
their mouths. The light through the leaves dimmed and disappeared, and they were left with the candle in the middle of
the table, the light coming through the partially opened back
door to the house.

"Dessert time," Charlie declared, and went into the house,
returning with a small plate of cinnamon-dusted cookies
and two small cups of thick, dark coffee. They ate and drank,
quieter now, watching the movements of each other's hands,
eyes.

"You know," she commented, taking a last sip of coffee,

"I've met a lot of guys who see sex like dessert—the prize you get after you eat all the vegetables that make the women happy.

"I guess I see it a little differently," she continued reflectively. "I think sex should be like dinner. And this is how I like to eat."

"THE MEAT IS DONE," Lillian pronounced, taking the spoon from Tom's idle hand and running it in a wide circle around the pan, pulling the sausage into the center, where it steamed and simmered.

"Now we're ready for the next step—but first a trick. A meat sauce loves red wine. But if we put in the red wine now, the meat will taste acidic, so we're going to add some milk." Lillian poured what seemed like a huge amount of white liquid into the mixture. "I know it seems odd, but trust me."

Tom looked down into the pan. It did look strange, the white at first swirling around the meat, pulling away from the oil like a finicky child who doesn't want to get her hands dirty. But as he watched, Tom saw the milk begin to enter the meat, change its color to an almost ashy gray, softening its edges.

"We'll let that simmer until the milk is absorbed," Lillian

commented. "I know," she acknowledged, "it all takes so much time. While you're waiting, you could answer three e-mails. You could call a friend, start the laundry. But tonight there is no time, so we don't need to worry about wasting it. You can just sit and let your thoughts unwind. And you'll be glad you did, because time will change the taste into something smooth—the difference between polyester and velvet."

TOM HAD STAYED at the restaurant only through the summer, making money to help pay for law school. He wanted Charlie to quit, too, and go back to school, but she wouldn't. The restaurant owner had had a change of philosophy, perhaps prompted by the meals Charlie kept leaving on his desk, and had offered her Tom's position when he found out Tom was going back to school in the fall.

"But do you want to work here all your life?" Tom asked her when she told him the news.

She looked at him, disappointed. "I want to cook," she said, "and this is the only restaurant in town, unless you count the fish-and-chips joint."

"What about your literature degree?" he persisted, caught up in the energy of his first week back at classes. "Don't you want to do something that lasts?"

She stared at him and shook her head. "Poetry isn't any different than food, Tom. We humans want to make things, and those things sink into us, whether we know it or not. Maybe your mind won't remember what I cooked last week, but your body will.

"And I have come to believe," she added, smiling wickedly, "that our bodies are far more intelligent than our brains."

There had never been a way to counter Charlie, perhaps because she didn't care if he agreed with her or not. She loved him, she knew that, and knew that he loved her.

"Why me?" he asked her, looking up at her face through the cascade of her hair falling about them.

"You're the oregano," she said simply.

"WE CAN ADD the wine now," Lillian prompted. The milk was gone, soaked into the meat. "Tom, will you get a bottle of red from the cook's shelf?" She turned to the class. "Now it might not seem to matter what wine goes in the sauce—it's going to simmer so long, anyway. But you'll notice the difference if you take care with the ingredients. We don't want to skimp on our wine, even if it's in a sauce, and we want a wine that can hold its own with the meat—something heavy and full and mellow."

Tom brought over a bottle and handed it to Lillian with questioning eyes. She pulled open the cork and breathed in, smiled.

"That'll do just fine," she said.

CHARLIE CALLED THEM "mamma wines," after the matrons they met in Italy on their honeymoon—a grand, two-week tour, celebrating his new job in a big-city law firm and the chance for Charlie to cook in a restaurant with a capital R. Their plan had been to start in Rome, and then move on to Florence, Lake Como, Venice. But Charlie reached their *agriturismo* forty-five minutes outside Rome and stopped.

"Taste this," she said during dinner at the long wooden table. "We aren't leaving until I know how to make this pasta."

Linguini led to ravioli followed by cannelloni, caponata. The town was small and unattractive, something Tom had believed was impossible in Italy. Its best function seemed to be as an overnight stop for slow tourists on their way between Rome and Florence. The buildings were post–World War II, concrete and stucco, not an arch, a fresco, a little-known Caravaggio to be found. When Tom tried to tell Charlie this, she just smiled and told him to go find a little hill town where he could taste wine, or something.

"I've got what I need," she would say, and then add with a grin, "at least for the morning." And she would head to the kitchen, where she would be greeted with choruses of "*La bella americana si è finalmente alzata dal letto*"—The beautiful American has finally gotten up out of bed—provoking roomfuls of knowing laughter.

Tom learned to be back for lunch at the long table under

the trees outside, and after lunch, when the farmhouse would settle into a profound quiet and Charlie would roll luxuriantly into his arms, her hair an ever-shifting maze of smells—fennel, nutmeg, sea salt. Hours later she would leave him and return to the women, only to start the whole process over again at dinner.

"You could have a worse honeymoon," she chided him, with a wink. "I could be pillaging some old museum for poems . . ."

He didn't care, he realized. Didn't care when reservations, so carefully made six months before, slipped by, and with them views of a terra-cotta-colored duomo, a Grand Canal, a foam-kissed cappuccino at a lakeside café. Every lunch, every dinner, he returned to a woman who seemed to draw into her body the very essence of the food she was learning to make, becoming deeper and more complicated and exciting.

After two weeks, they left and returned to Rome. Charlie spent the plane flight home scribbling designs, notes for ravioli recipes, on scraps of paper. "What would you think if I tried bourbon in the filling?" she would ask him. "Italy meets the Deep South."

Back at home she found a job at a restaurant, and within weeks her new dishes were finding their way onto the menu. Some evenings Tom went to the restaurant at the end of his work day and ate with her on the back steps; some nights they both knew in advance he would simply go home. He would open the door of their house to the smell of sauce on the back burner. By the pan, there was always a note.

Hey, Darling,

I'm working late, so you'll have to use those beautiful hands of yours in a useful occupation for once. Cook the pasta. Don't ask what's in the sauce. We'll see if it had the particular effect I wanted later.

I love you,

Charlie

"You could sit here all evening and watch the meat absorb the wine," Lillian commented. "It's amazing what you'll end up thinking about. Plate tectonics. A child in your lap. Crocuses.

"For now, however, we'll add the tomatoes and move on to the pasta. Now, we want some tomatoes for texture. You could use a can of crushed tomatoes, but crushed tomatoes are made from the bits, the parts nobody is going to see anyway. If you want to make sure you have the best, then you buy them whole and crush them yourself. Again, more time." Lillian opened a can of whole tomatoes and pulled out a Cuisinart from the shelves under the counter. She ladled tomatoes from the can; the machine whirred, and then stopped. Lillian tipped its con-tents into the pan.

"Finally, a bit of tomato sauce to thicken things up." Lillian opened a can of tomato sauce and poured some in. "There. That can take care of itself for a while," she said, turning down the heat under the pan.

"Now, on to the pasta." Lillian pulled out a large container of flour and plunked it onto the countertop.

"You could use dry—it would work just fine. But we have time tonight. So, go ahead and put some of that in a mound," she directed Tom. "Then make a hollow in the middle. Use your hands."

Tom reached into the wide mouth of the glass jar and felt the flour between his fingers, soft as feathers. He cupped his palm and pulled up a handful, then another and another, creating a small mountain on the wooden countertop. He made an indentation in the center, running the base of his thumb along the edges to smooth them out, feeling the flour shift beneath his fingertips; it reminded him of playing at the beach, hours with the sun on his back and acres of building materials at his disposal.

"Good." Lillian went to the refrigerator and returned with a small bowl of eggs. She cracked one into the hollow. "We add the eggs one at a time until it seems as if there is enough," she said. "Tom, you can stir with a fork—you'll want to make sure there are no lumps."

It was Tom who had found the lump, nestled like a marble at the base of Charlie's breast. His breathing, which had been racing to keep up with his excitement, suddenly stopped. It was like waking to a gun in his face; the world held, mid-fall.

"Hey, bud, where did you go?" Charlie had asked him teasingly.

He had pulled himself up even closer to her, his lips against the line of her jaw. He took her hand and led her fingers to the lump. Then he drew his head back and fell into the look in her eyes.

"THAT'S ENOUGH," Lillian said, taking the fork from Tom's hand. "Now we work the dough. Think of your hands as waves moving in and out of the ocean. You fold the dough over, then push it gently with the heel of your hand, then fold again and push again, for as long as it takes until the dough feels as if it is part of you. You could use a dough hook on your mixer if you wanted, but you'd miss out on something. Kneading dough is like swimming or walking—it keeps part of your mind busy and allows the rest of your mind to go where it wants or needs to."

TWO WEEKS AFTER he found the lump, Tom came home from work early and heard laughter at the back of the house— Charlie's and a man's he didn't recognize. He walked into the kitchen and saw Charlie sitting at the table, her shirt open, breasts falling forward unrestrained. Her head was tipped back, laughter floating up from her like flowers. At her feet knelt a man he hadn't seen before.

"What..." Tom stood unmoving, not understanding.

"Tom," said Charlie, smiling up at him, "meet Remy. He's helping me with a little project."

She looked at Tom's expression and laughed softly. "Remy blows glass, Tom. We're taking a mold of my breasts. Remy's going to blow me a pair of wineglasses. One for me and one for you—we never had quite such an equal distribution before." She was still laughing, but her eyes were on his, waiting for understanding.

Tom looked at his wife and the man on the floor, his hands cupped around her breasts. Charlie's words fell about him, and he realized he had no way to make sense of the information he was being given.

Charlie watched him, took a breath, and the laughter swept off her face like dust in front of a broom. "Tom, we both know what the doctors are going to say tomorrow. They're going to take my breasts. I don't care, they can have them, but I want something." She shook her head. "Something I can hold in my hand. Do you understand?"

Tom looked at the woman he loved and the man kneeling on the floor. He walked over and put his hand softly on Remy's shoulder. Then he bent over and kissed his wife.

. . .

OVER THE FOLLOWING MONTHS, the world turned into some-thing small and terrifying, with its own language of terminol-ogy and statistics, prognoses and theories made from the very stuff of reality—although Tom often thought that Charlie's beliefs about yeast or spices were more worth putting your faith in. He found himself yearning for days of grocery lists and difficult clients, things you could complain about because you knew they would eventually go away.

One night he came home from work to find the kitchen empty, the door to the backyard open. Tom couldn't see Charlie at first, but then he spotted the gentle motion of the hammock, the slightest of movements under the apple trees. As he went down the stairs he could see Charlie's profile, her cheekbones, sharp in the light, the inch or so of hair that was beginning to grow back along her skull. She had been worried about her looks, she who had been the object of so many appreciative glances, and yet her beauty had not so much changed with the loss of her hair and breasts and all the weight, but distilled, intensified—so pure and personal he sometimes felt as if he should ask permission to look at her.

"You know," Charlie said, without turning her head, "one of the unanticipated benefits of big breasts is that they make very large wineglasses." She raised her glass, one of the pair Remy had made.

"Charlie, should you be . . . ?" Charlie turned toward him, and the expression in her eyes stopped his words.

"It's a nice evening, don't you think?" Charlie said. "It deserves a good red."

"Charlie . . . ?" He waited, holding on to the air in his lungs, knowing that with the next breath everything would be different.

"New nurse," Charlie replied, taking a long, reflective sip of wine, "wanted to make sure she was doing her job well— thought I'd appreciate those lab results today, not wait until the doctor's appointment."

"But I thought . . ."

"Apparently not," she said, shaking her head slightly. "Want some wine? I saved some for you."

She shifted position, making space in the hammock next to her. Tom climbed in, Charlie holding the glass high above her head to minimize the motion of the wine. They lay, looking across the length of the hammock at each other. It was quiet in the yard, the noise of the traffic out on the street and the sounds of their neighbors arriving home enclosing the space like a blanket.

"You know," she said after a time, leaning her face against his leg, "every night, people used to come into my restaurant and I would watch them as they ate my food. They'd relax, they'd talk, they'd remember who they were. Maybe they went home and made love. All I know is I was part of that. I was a part of them.

"A very quiet part." She smiled. "But I'm starting to think there are advantages to quiet."

He looked at her across the hammock. She was already leaving, a bit at a time. He longed to reach for her, pull her across the length of the hammock to him, but the still, quiet look in her eyes stopped him.

"They aren't taking any more of you," he said. "I'm not going to let it happen."

"My sweet lawyer," she said, her voice deep and slow as the bottom of a river, "I don't think you have a choice." She paused, and took another sip of wine. "We're all just ingredients, Tom. What matters is the grace with which you cook the meal."

"WHEN THE DOUGH IS READY," Lillian said, "we roll it out and cut it, into long, thin strips. There are machines that do this— try them if you'd like. Or find yourself a long wooden rolling pin, a sharp knife, and a good, tall chair to hang the strips over. They won't all look the same, and that's all right. It's your hands that matter."

OVER THE WEEKS, Charlie disappeared, as steadily as water evaporating from a boiling kettle. Watched pots, Tom thought, and took a leave from his work to sit with her, his eyes never leaving the ever-deepening curves of her face, the tips of his fingers resting next to hers when her skin could no longer tolerate touch.

"Isn't that a bitch," she said, with her slow, steady smile, "just when you most wanted to jump my bones."

And he couldn't tell her that he did, he would, that he would take whatever of her was left. Instead he commandeered every part of her care that required touch, washing her by hand when she could no longer stand in the shower, massaging lotion into her feet and legs and hands when the medications sucked the moisture from her skin, buzz-cutting her hair when it grew past her self-imposed one-inch limit.

"Bloody hell, Tom," she said, "at least I shouldn't have to worry about my hair. You think people really won't know I'm sick?"

And he learned to cook, whatever she could eat, adding the subtle and gentle spices that gave flavor without attacking her decimated stomach lining, the greens and yellows and reds that brought the outside world to her.

"Promise me you'll keep cooking when I'm gone." Charlie's voice was insistent.

"I'll eat," he said, frustrated. "Don't worry about me."

"Not just eat," Charlie corrected him. "Cook."

Finally, even food was no longer a topic. The house lost the smells of cooking and Charlie lived only on air and water, diving deep into her mind for longer and longer periods of time, coming back only to look into him, as if her eyes could tell him everything she had seen while she was gone. Then one day she met his eyes, dove, and simply disappeared. Tom was left behind in a stunning vacuum, surrounded by stacks of useless medications and bandages, holding only a feeling, deeply lodged in his bones, his brain, his heart, that even though Charlie had told him again and again that it wasn't about winning, he had lost.

After the weeks and months of watching, of life suspended in the bottomless well of Charlie's illness, the world seemed absurdly practical. There were bills to pay, a lawn to mow, laundry that smelled only of sweat and last night's microwaved dinner. Incoming phone calls reverted to casual check-ins from friends; no longer was he the source of grim updates. The hand-delivered meals from helpful neighbors slowed and then disappeared. He went to the grocery store without wondering if she would be there when he returned, the churning in his stomach replaced by a more certain and deeper ache. She was nowhere and everywhere, and he couldn't stop looking.

The only people who really wanted to talk about Charlie's death were the service providers and government agencies, who all wanted proof, in hard copy. He became the dispenser of death certificates, sending forth missives of mortality to phone service providers, credit card companies, life and health insurance, the Department of Motor Vehicles and Social Security. It was amazing, he thought, how many people cared to know, for sure, that you were dead.

Charlie had been clear that she didn't want to be buried. "Not unless you can turn me into compost," she told him firmly, then explained to him what she wanted. So one night a group of friends gathered and ate dinner on the beach that Charlie loved—slices of dripping cantaloupe from the old fruit vendor who cried when he heard the news, fresh fish marinated in olive oil and tarragon and grilled over a beachfront fire, chunks of thick-crusted bread from her favorite bakery in town, a spice cake Tom made from Charlie's own recipe. Afterward, they threw her ashes in great arcs out to the water. What only Tom knew was that each of them carried a tiny bit of her home with them that night, baked into the cake they had eaten.

After that, Tom stopped talking. It was as if all those conversations, the hard ones while she was alive and the prosaic ones after her death, had used up anything he would ever want to say. It was simply too much trouble to open his mouth, to think about what someone else might want or need to hear. His mind was busy, although he couldn't have told anyone with what.

ALMOST NINE MONTHS LATER, on what would have been Charlie's birthday, a friend had taken him to Lillian's restaurant for dinner. "Charlie would want you to be around food on her birthday, buddy," he had said, "and Lillian's will make even you want to eat."

It was August, the leaves on the cherry trees in the restau-rant garden green and full when they walked up the path to Lillian's. They sat on the porch in the large Adirondack chairs with glasses of red wine as they waited for a table, listening to the hum of conversation about them, the clink of silverware coming through the open windows of the dining room inside. Tom felt his mind slowing, coming to rest in the serenity of the garden surrounding them.

When they were finally seated in the wood-paneled dining room, a waitress came up to their table and greeted them.

"We have a wonderful seafood special tonight," she announced. "Lillian found beautiful fresh clams and mussels at the seafood market today and she is serving them over homemade angel hair pasta in a sauce of butter, garlic, and wine, with just a bit of red pepper flakes and . . ." The waitress stopped, flustered at her lack of memory.

"Oregano," Tom said quietly.

"Yes," the waitress responded, relieved. "Thank you. How did you know?"

"Lucky guess," Tom said, raising his glass in a silent toast. He looked down at the table in front of him, concentrating on the weave of the linen cloth, the curve of the handle of his fork, the cut-glass lines of the small, round bowl filled with sea salt and fennel.

Then Tom noticed a folded chocolate-colored placard, almost hidden behind the bowl of salt. He picked up the small sign and read the cream-colored script flowing across the surface.

Announcing:
The new session of
The School of Essential Ingredients

"CLASS, I think we are ready," Lillian called over her shoulder, as she emptied the pasta from the huge pot into a colander. "Now all we need are plates."

As Lillian transferred the steaming spaghetti noodles from the colander to a heavy ceramic bowl, the students stood up obediently and went to the shelves, passing white pasta plates from one person to the next like a fireman's brigade. They lined up in front of the counter, jokingly jostling each other. Lillian carried over the big blue bowl and began placing a serving of pasta on each plate.

"Tom," she said, turning to him, "you do the honors with the sauce. It's yours, after all." She watched as he ladled the first fragrant red spoonful onto a waiting bed of creamy-yellow pasta. When everyone was served, the class settled into groups in the chairs, talking companionably before taking their first bites, after which the room dissolved into a silence interrupted only by the sounds of forks against plates and the occasional sigh of satisfaction.

"Look at what you did," Lillian remarked quietly, standing next to Tom at the counter.

"They'll eat it," he said, "and then it'll be gone."

"That's what makes it a gift," Lillian replied.

Chloe

C hloe had met Jake at the bar and grill where she got her first job, bussing tables. Bussing wasn't what she had set out to do, but when you've just graduated from high school and don't know how you'd pay for college even if your father thought you could get in, bussing tables can seem like a good option. Unless you have a tendency to drop things, which Chloe did.

She was sitting on the back stoop of the restaurant, crying her way through her fifteen-minute lunch break when she felt someone drop down on the step beside her, and smelled meat, fresh off the grill.

"Thought you might need this," said Jake, handing her a burger. Chloe stared at him. Jake was tall, with that black-cat grace reserved for grill cooks and high school athletes, and curls that tangled their way lazily down his neck to his collar. As a cook, he was supposed to wear a hair net, but people didn't tell Jake things like that. Jake was the guy, the one all the waitresses hoped would snap their orders down off the revolving cook's wheel, not just because he was gorgeous, but because he could turn around four burgers, a fish sandwich, a Caesar salad, and a clam-sauce pasta for that seven-top you forgot about until they grabbed your elbow and asked where their food was and said it better be there in the next five minutes or they were walking out, and with Jake you knew that in four and a half minutes there you would be with all those plates balanced up your arm like a conga line, smiling like God just blessed you personally, and pulling in the tip of your lifetime.

But Jake didn't usually have anything to do with bussers. Bussers brought back the dirty dishes, the leftovers that told the cooks how good the food was or wasn't that night. As far as Chloe could tell, bussers were just hands to the cooks, and ears to the waitresses who filled them with one harshly whispered diatribe after another.

"So, which of the prom princesses was it tonight?" Jake asked, grinning.

"What do you mean?"

"Someone got you crying. My money's on a waitress." He saw the expression on her face. "Don't worry, I'm not telling. You know that wall in the kitchen between the cooks and the waitresses? I don't owe anything to the other side."

Chloe ate a bite of the hamburger. It was good, and messy. She wiped her mouth with the back of her hand. "Cynthia," she said, "I knocked over a wineglass at one of her tables."

What she didn't mention was Cynthia's prolonged discussion of Chloe's ineptitude and likely dismal love life, along with something about "cleaning that black crap off your eyes while you're at it."

"Ah, the queen herself." Jake's smile came at you sideways, like a car speeding through a four-way stop. "Just don't bus her tables for a while. She'll get the message."

Chloe considered discussing with Jake the vertebrae that would be required for such an undertaking, but Jake was already standing up.

"Time to get back in there. You, too, I bet. Stick around when you're done. There's a group of us who hang out after work."

Chloe nodded, unable to speak.

Four weeks later she moved out of her parents' house and into Jake's apartment.

LIVING WITH JAKE hadn't been quite what she expected, although she didn't really know what that was, either. For the first week or two she felt like a prom queen herself. When Jake worked the late shift, he would bring home food from the middle page of the menu—the steaks and prawns and sauté dishes that were off the list of busser-appropriate food, items found on the back page under "Sandwiches and Other Light Fare." Jake would wake her up and feed her with his fingers, accidentally dripping sauce on her so he could lick it off, leading to all sorts of activities that left Chloe exhausted and more prone to dropping things than ever, including a particularly spectacular display of cascading silverware one Thursday evening.

The manager stopped her as she was leaving work that night.

"So, Chloe," he said, "how are things working out for you?"

Chloe may not have gone to college, but she knew a rhetorical question when she heard one.

"You know, Jake's a friend of mine," the manager told her soothingly. "I'll give you a good reference."

And thus started Chloe's next six months as a busser at the Bombay Grill, the Green Door, Babushka, Sartoro's. With each transition, she felt Jake's enthusiasm for her weaken, along with her own confidence. The bed feasts diminished over the months; he rarely woke her up when he returned, which wasn't always. His comments became increasingly sarcastic, noting with regularity the times she tripped or knocked a glass with her elbow.

"It'll help you," he said. "This is a habit you have to break."

Chloe looked to see if the pun was intentional, but apparently it wasn't.

. . .

IT HAD BEEN on Chloe's last, memorable night at Sartoro's that she ran into Lillian. Chloe stepped back, horrified, watching the water from the three glasses she had been carrying land in a deluge on Lillian's shoes, followed in rapid succession by Chloe's apologies.

Lillian smiled and reached into her purse. She handed Chloe a chocolate-colored business card with "Lillian's" and a telephone number written in luxurious white script across the front.

"Just in case," she said, and then shook off her shoes and returned to her table.

When Chloe had called the number three days later, mortified, but in need of a new job, Lillian answered the phone.

"This is Chloe, the busser with the water glasses . . . ?"

"Yes, Chloe, I remember. How about you come by Monday evening, at five?"

"You want to hire me? But I'm clumsy, you saw."

"I'm not so sure about the clumsy part." Lillian's voice danced like water running over rocks. "And by the way, I didn't say I'd hire you, did I? See you at five o'clock."

WHEN CHLOE showed up that Monday, the lights were on in the dining room, but it was empty. She walked up the four front steps, listening to the slight creak in the wood, feeling for the welcoming give in the tread she hoped would be there.

At the door, she knocked, feeling a little silly—it was a restaurant, after all—but there was something so private about the place that her hand simply refused to turn the knob without announcing her presence.

Lillian answered the door and ushered her inside. "Welcome," she said. "What do you think of my restaurant?"

Chloe looked around at the tables, curled into corners, their linens white and starched and heavy, the candlesticks solid and silver. The wood floor under her feet was burnished brown and smooth from wear; the walls above the wainscoting were adorned with hand-painted plates and etchings of small towns that looked European, although Chloe couldn't be sure.

"It's beautiful," Chloe said, "but can I ask why you might want me to work for you? Here?"

"Well, let's just say that in my experience people who seem distracted can be some of the most interesting people you'll ever meet."

"Nobody's ever put it that way before."

"It all depends on what happens when you do pay attention."

"How do you think you'll get me to do that? I mean, my boyfriend already yells at me every time I drop something."

"How does that work?"

"Not well." Chloe smiled in spite of herself.

"Then I suppose we'll have to try something else. Do you want to?"

"Yes." Chloe's voice surprised her in its intensity.

"All right, then. I want you to learn this room—whatever

that means to you. I'll be back in five minutes." Lillian went through the kitchen door and disappeared.

Chloe stared after her, still wondering where the rest of the staff were, when the people might arrive, why there was no noise in the kitchen.

"By the way," Lillian's voice came from the kitchen, "we're closed on Monday nights, so take your time. And don't be afraid to touch."

Chloe looked at the table in front of her, and then reached down to stroke the crisp finish of the linen cloth cascading off the table. She picked up the fragile flute of a pre-dinner Prosecco glass, its stem a slim twig between her fingers, and set it down again carefully. She walked to the next table, listening to the sound her feet made sliding across the wood floor, then walked to the window to look out to the garden, lit up by the last of the evening's light, so that the roses seemed to glow and the leaves of cherry trees took on a sharp-edged definition. She lifted one of the chairs by the window table quietly and pulled it back, then sat down, looking across the room.

Lillian walked in and Chloe started to her feet.

"No," said Lillian. "That's the right thing to do. You want to know where you work."

"I love it here," Chloe said, then stopped.

"Then you'll be careful," Lillian said.

"I don't know if I can. What if I break things? I couldn't stand it."

"Okay, let's try this. Close your eyes and walk to the kitchen door."

Chloe could think of many reasons why this was one of the more questionable requests anyone had ever made of her. But Lillian seemed completely unconcerned about the hundreds, probably thousands, of dollars that stood between Chloe and the door to the kitchen. So after a minute, with Lillian still patiently waiting, Chloe decided it was Lillian's crystal and china after all, and she closed her eyes and began sliding her feet along the wooden floor, very, very slowly.

"You can go more quickly," Lillian said, to her right. "You know where you're going."

And Chloe realized she did. There was the two-top near Lillian, the one closest to the front door, but next to the window that looked out to the front porch and beyond to the garden that led to the gate. There was the four-top on her left in the middle of the room, that should have felt exposed but didn't because the lighting was softer, and there was, yes she remembered it, a chair that had been pulled out just a bit, so she moved a little closer to the two-top, feeling her fingers run across the top of a chair and out into the space where the front door would open. From there, it was a matter of going mostly forward, but weaving a bit to the right and left—you could tell, Chloe realized, when you were closer to a table because of the smell of candles and starch, and the little white bowls of spiced salt that released just the lightest touch of fennel into the air. And then, she was at the kitchen door.

"It's not such a big room, after all," Lillian commented.

"I want to work here," Chloe said, simply. "I won't drop a thing."

It had been a couple of months later that Chloe saw lights on in the restaurant kitchen on a Monday night when she walked past on her way home from the grocery store. The next afternoon when she arrived at work, Chloe asked Lillian about the activity in the kitchen.

"That's my cooking class," Lillian replied. "I teach lessons the first Monday of the month."

"Could I come?"

"Chloe, if you want to work in the kitchen, I can start you as a prep cook."

"I don't want it as a job," Chloe fumbled. "That's what my boyfriend does. I'd just like to be able to cook sometimes. So when he comes home from work, I could do that."

Lillian nodded. "I see. Well, a new class is starting in September. You could give it a try."

"What do the classes cost?" Chloe was running numbers in her head. She wanted this to be a surprise, but didn't know if she could afford it, and didn't know how many extra shifts she could add to her schedule without Jake noticing.

"Let's just call it on-the-job training for now, shall we?"

· · ·

THE FIRST NIGHT of classes Chloe had realized quickly that she was at least a decade younger than anyone else in the room, which did nothing to reduce her sense of trepidation. Lillian saw her from across the kitchen and smiled but made no move to introduce her to any of the students. Chloe went over to the sink to wash her hands, and stood next to a fragile-looking woman with silver hair.

"Are you here with someone?" the woman asked conversationally. "Your mother, perhaps?"

"No," said Chloe, a bit defiantly.

The woman regarded her appraisingly. "Good for you," she said. "My name is Isabelle."

Chloe hadn't been sure that she could kill a crab that first night, but she took a cue from her experiment walking across the dining room and closed her eyes. In the darkened space of her mind, she had felt the life in the crab under her fingers, and mourned its end, simply and deeply, before pulling off the shell as quickly as she could. When she ate the crab later she closed her eyes again, and felt the life come into her.

At the end of the class, Lillian touched her elbow as she left. "You're learning, Chloe. You should be proud of yourself."

While Chloe loved the classes and the people in them, she hadn't had the courage to try any of the lessons at home until after Tom's night with the pasta. Chloe had watched him, the gentleness on his face as he worked, the way his hands touched the ingredients like the body of someone he cherished, and she decided this would be the dish she would make for Jake, and he would see her food as love.

It was harder getting along with Jake these days. Even though she was holding on to a regular job, the river of his commentary did not cease; it simply changed its course. Her hair (she was thinking of going natural; he thought brown was boring), her clothes (not seductive enough for him, too risqué for the outside world), her ideas (nonexistent). Sometimes Chloe felt as if he was tying her up into a tight little ball, small enough to throw far away from him.

It took Chloe a week to get up the courage, and the money, to make the pasta sauce—she wanted to buy a real red wine, deep and strong but gentle on the heart; Lillian had said that the sauce would follow the lead of the wine. Still, after all her thought, she had to ask Lillian to buy the wine for her, as she was too young to make the purchase herself.

"I have a better idea," Lillian remarked. "Come with me."

The two of them contemplated the restaurant wine rack. "You know," Lillian commented with a rueful smile, "I could get in a lot of trouble doing this. Perhaps if I just give this to you we can deem it culinary encouragement." She pulled a bottle from the rack, wiped the label, and presented it to Chloe.

"Please put this somewhere in the bottom of that backpack of yours, will you? I'd hate to lose my liquor license."

AT HER APARTMENT, Chloe unpacked the wine and the canned tomatoes, the meat and the bouillon cubes. The garlic had been dusty black with mold at the supermarket, so she had decided to try the produce stand. It was cold outside, and the produce stand was a half-mile toward the other side of town, but she felt full of energy at the thought of the meal she would prepare. Chloe left the apartment, wrapping a scarf around her neck and pulling it up to her nose, breathing in her own moisture, the cold tickling her eyelashes.

She reached the stand, stamping the blood back into her feet, and entered into the relative warmth of the fabric-sided enclosure. After the winter outside, it was a carnival of life, mounds of green peppers and red apples, neon oranges, spiky-edged artichokes and furry little kiwis. She found the garlic but couldn't resist a round red tomato that looked as if it had just been pulled from the vine.

The shop owner approached her. "Can I help you?" he asked, a bit warily. There was a high school nearby; the fruit stand was a logical destination for a five-finger lunch.

Chloe, caught up in the red depths of the tomato, missed the admonishment in his voice and turned with a smile. "Where did you get such a beautiful tomato?"

The shop owner's face relaxed. "I grew it myself, indoors," he said. "I only bring in a few of them."

"I'm making a special tomato sauce today," Chloe explained, pride and embarrassment mixed in her voice. Then she saw his face. "Oh, no, I wouldn't put this in the sauce." She tried to fig-ure out how to explain. "It's just to help me remember why."

The shop owner regarded her appraisingly. "It's yours," he said with a nod. "The garlic, you can pay for."

WHEN CHLOE had come back into the apartment, she could smell meat cooking. Jake was standing at the stove, watching the frying pan.

"Hey, thanks for picking up groceries," he exclaimed. "Burgers will be ready in a couple minutes."

"I was going to make pasta . . ." Chloe stopped.

"Oh, that'll take too much time." He saw her looking at the open bottle in his hand. "Good wine, babe, thanks," he com-mented, taking a drink. "Are you trying to butter me up for Valentine's Day?"

Chloe shook her head. "I'll be right back. I have to do something."

"Well, hurry, the burgers are almost ready."

Chloe went downstairs and around to the back of the apart-ment building. She stood with her back against the wall, breathing hard.

"Stupid girl," she muttered to herself. "What did you think was going to happen?"

Then she lifted the lid of the huge blue rubbish bin and threw in the small paper bag she had been holding.

THE NEXT NIGHT at work, Chloe had broken two wineglasses and put a cutting knife in the pot sink full of water. When the dishwasher yanked his hand out and let loose a veritable paella of Spanish invective, Lillian pulled Chloe aside.

"*Now* you aren't paying attention."

Chloe looked at her, panicked. "Please don't fire me."

"I'm not firing you, Chloe. I'm paying attention to you. This is what that looks like. Can you do that for me tonight?"

Chloe nodded.

"And make sure you come to class on Monday."

WHEN CHLOE ARRIVED on Monday night, she saw the rest of the students waiting outside. A few moments later, Lillian ran up the walk toward them, several brown paper bags in her hands, her hair loose and flying behind her.

"Sorry I'm late," she called out. "I had to get a few things together."

She wound her way through the assembled group, greeting each person as she went past, and unlocked the kitchen, flicking on the lights with her thumb as she entered. The students took their seats, Chloe by chance ending up next to Antonia.

"Now"—Lillian placed the bags on the wooden counter and turned to the class—"I have something special planned for tonight. We've done several more complicated dinners recently. But one of the essential lessons in cooking is how extraordinary the simplest foods can be when they are prepared with care and the freshest ingredients. So tonight, while it is cold and blustery outside, we are going to experience some utterly uncomplicated bliss."

There was a knock on the kitchen door. The students looked at it in surprise.

"Perfect timing." Lillian went to open the door. Outside was a woman with bronzed, wrinkled skin and white, white hair. What she had gained in age, she appeared to have lost in height, reaching at most to Lillian's shoulder.

"Class," said Lillian, smiling, "this is my friend Abuelita. She is here to help us tonight."

Abuelita entered the room and looked over the rows of students. "Thank you for having me," she said, her voice warm and gravelly with age. "You must be a special class—Lillian has never asked me to help her teach before. Or perhaps she is just getting old and lazy." And then she winked.

Antonia leaned over toward Chloe. "She reminds me of

my *nonna*. Maybe she will tell us secrets about Lillian." Chloe stared at Antonia—she had always viewed the young woman, with her effortless olive beauty and her accent that seemed to invite men to bed, as something to be observed in pristinely silent awe—but Antonia still gazed at her, mischief flickering in her eyes, and Chloe found herself grinning.

"Like why she never got married . . ." she suggested.

"Or where she lives," Isabelle whispered, leaning forward conspiratorially.

"Enough chatter out there," Lillian said, amused. "Chloe, you seem to have plenty of energy tonight; why don't you come up and help us?"

Chloe started to shake her head, but Antonia gave her a supportive push on the back of her shoulder.

"Go on. You should do this."

Chloe walked up to the counter and stood a bit apart from Lillian and Abuelita.

"Abuelita was my first cooking teacher, and she showed me how to make tortillas," Lillian explained. "Now, if we were really authentic"—Lillian made a slight bow in Abuelita's direction—"we would have made the *masa* ourselves. We would have soaked and cooked dried corn in water and powdered lime to make *nixtamal*, which we would then have ground into the *masa harina*—luckily for us, Abuelita has a wonderful store where you can buy the flour already made."

"When I was a girl," Abuelita commented, "it was my job

to grind the corn. We had a big stone, with a dip in the middle, called a *metate*, and I would kneel in front of it and use a *mano*—like a rolling pin made of stone. It takes a long time to make enough for one tortilla, you know, and you need strong arms. And knees. It is much easier this way," she said, picking up the bag of *masa harina* and pouring a yellow stream of corn flour into the bowl.

"Now add some water," she said, handing Chloe the bowl.

"How much?" Chloe asked.

Abuelita's eyes moved over Chloe, her sweatshirt baggy on her slim shoulders, her eyes dark with liner. She shrugged, a movement as light and casual as wind over grass.

"Do what makes sense."

Chloe threw a despairing look at Antonia and Isabelle, who gestured encouragement, and then she took the bowl to the sink and turned on the tap, feeling the soft grains between her fingers turn cold and slick under the stream of water. She shut off the faucet, mixing the liquid into the flour with her hands. Still too dry. She added a bit more water, mixed again, added a little more, finally feeling the two elements become one.

"I get it," she said, looking up at Abuelita.

"Good," said Abuelita. "Now, take some dough and make a ball." Her hands lifted a bit of the mixture and rolled it between her palms, her movements fluid and assured, as the students watched her. "Then you pat it," she said, the ball passing between her palms, flattening within the motion of her hands. She paused for a moment, curling the tips of her fingers, then rotated the dough in a circular motion, pulling the edges out, creating an even, round shape, then returned to patting, rhythmically, quickly.

"It's like watching a waterfall," Carl commented appreciatively from the back row.

"They say," noted Lillian, "that it takes thirty-two pats to make a tortilla."

Abuelita chuckled, never slowing in her movements. "Such precision from a woman who doesn't believe in recipes."

"Not that *she* does, either," retorted Lillian.

"When it's important." Abuelita put down the finished tortilla, then took some more dough from the bowl and handed it to Chloe. "Now you try."

Chloe hesitantly rolled it between her palms. "It's like Play-Doh," she commented, "only softer." She began flipping the ball from hand to hand, pushing the shape flat. After a time, she looked down at the dough in dismay, the edges splayed out and separated like ragged flower petals, the thickness irregular, lumpy. She rolled it up and started patting again, determinedly.

"This is not baseball," said Abuelita after a time, but kindly. "Be calm." She took Chloe's hands in her own, stilling them. "Think of a dance with someone you love. You want to stay close to each other. You don't need to think about anything else."

Chloe began again, slowly. She felt the ball of dough shifting back and forth, back and forth. Gradually, she felt the shape opening up, spreading out like another hand, warm from her own, slipping across the slim space between her palms. She quickened her pace. The rhythm was soothing, the sound of her hands like raindrops falling down a gutter.

"I think that is good," said Abuelita after a minute or so.

Chloe looked down to see the finished tortilla in her hand. "That was amazing," she said to Abuelita. "Can everyone try?"

Abuelita handed her the bowl and Chloe walked along the rows of students. Each of them made a small ball and began patting, laughing at their mistakes, then gaining a rhythm, the sound of their hands turning into a muted, collective ovation.

"Now, there *are* tortilla presses," Lillian said. From under the counter she took out a metal object, two round circles connected by a hinge. She opened and closed it to show where the dough would go, how it would flatten under the pressure of the upper lid. "But I think every day deserves applause."

"And maybe a dance? Did you know this woman can dance?" Abuelita asked the class, eyes sparkling.

"Which leads us to salsa," Lillian said briskly, lifting a brown paper bag onto the counter. "Antonia," she said, cutting off the question Chloe could see forming on Antonia's lips, "could you come up and help Abuelita cook the tortillas while Chloe and I chop?

"Here you go," she said to Chloe, handing her a sharp knife.

"You want me to use this?" Chloe said in an undertone to Lillian. "You know me and knives." Lillian simply nodded.

Over by the hot griddle, Abuelita was explaining the cooking process to Antonia. "About half a minute on each side. They should puff up into little balloons—if they don't, you can press on them lightly with two fingers before you turn them."

Lillian pulled an item from her bag and put it in Chloe's hand. "Here," she said, "start with this."

The tomato was unlike anything Chloe had seen before, bulbous and swollen, more horizontal than vertical, with ridges running from top to bottom along its sides, straining in places, ready to burst. There was red, certainly, but of a painter's palette of variations, deep garnet to almost orange, with streaks of green and yellow. Its comforting weight filled her hand, the ridges sliding between her fingers. She pressed softly, then stopped, feeling the skin begin to depress beneath her touch.

"This is called an heirloom tomato," Lillian explained to the class. "Usually that's something you only get in August and September, but we were lucky today."

The air was beginning to fill with the sweet spiciness of roasting corn, the soft whispers of the tortillas flipping, then landing on the grill, the murmured conversation between Abuelita and Antonia, something about grandmothers, it sounded like. Chloe placed the tomato on the chopping block. She was surprised to find how much affection she had for its odd lumpiness. She tested the point of the knife, and the surface gave way quickly and cleanly, exposing the dense interior, juices dripping out onto the wooden board, along with a few seeds. Grasping the knife firmly, she drew it in a smooth, consistent stroke across the arc of the tomato, a slice falling neatly to one side.

"Good," Lillian remarked, and Chloe continued, slice after slice, amazed at her ability to create six divisions across the single fruit in front of her, then take the slices and turn them into small, neat squares.

"Time for a break." Abuelita brought Chloe a tortilla from the griddle. "Hold it in the flat of your hand," she directed, "now rub the end of the stick of butter across it and sprinkle on some salt." Chloe lifted the tortilla to her mouth, inhaling the round, warm smell of corn and melting butter, soft as a mother's hand moving across the back of her almost sleeping child.

"Why would you ever want to eat anything else?" Chloe asked as she finished.

"Maybe salsa," Lillian remarked, handing Chloe the cilantro, dripping with water.

WHEN IT WAS mixed together, the salsa was a celebration of red and white and green, cool and fresh and alive. On a tortilla, with a bit of crumbled white *queso fresco*, it was both satisfying

and invigorating, full of textures and adventures, like childhood held in your hand.

Chloe held her tortilla over a small plate, watching the drips
from the tomato juice and butter land on the white china. The
class was quiet, absorbed in the food in their hands. Abuelita
and Lillian stood at the counter, leaning into each other, talking
quietly, while Antonia removed the last of the tortillas from
the griddle and placed them on the stack underneath a white
kitchen towel to stay warm.

It was like a picture, Chloe thought. A recipe without
words. She stood still, sensing the kitchen around her, feeling the energy the room held, would hold until the next afternoon when the cooks and bussers and patrons arrived and it
would again become something more than the accumulation
of its bustle and ingredients, and the food they cooked would
become laughter and romance, warm and bright and golden.
She smiled.

Lillian walked over and pulled one last tomato from the bag
and handed it to Chloe. "I think you earned this," she said.

CLASS WAS OVER. Abuelita had gone home, claiming with a
laugh that she was too old for late hours. The others had left one
or a few at a time, Claire begging some tortillas to take home to
her children, Ian dragging Tom outside saying he wanted to ask
him a question, Helen and Carl offering Isabelle a ride.

It was quiet in the kitchen, the only sounds the rattling of the bowls as Chloe put them away, the swish of the towel as Lillian cleaned the last of the counters. The door clicked shut behind Antonia as she carried the last of the wooden folding chairs to the storage shed just outside.

"Can I ask you something?" Chloe met Antonia at the door as she reentered.

"*Certo.*" Of course.

"You are so beautiful," Chloe stumbled. "I'm not . . ."

"Ahhh . . ." Antonia smiled and turned to Lillian. "Can we borrow your restroom for a moment?" Lillian nodded, and Antonia grabbed a clean kitchen towel and took Chloe by the hand, leading her through the restaurant dining room and into the tiny green women's restroom. Standing in front of the mirror, Antonia took the clip that had been holding the waves of her black hair, and then deftly pulled Chloe's brown curls away from her face.

"Good," said Antonia, as she secured the clip in Chloe's hair. "Now, water."

"What?"

"Your face, please." She turned on the hot water.

Chloe filled her cupped hands with warm water and brought it up to her face. She could feel the heat meeting her skin, the smell, slightly metallic, green as the room around her. It was quiet in the space created between her hands and face, clean, safe.

"Now soap."

Chloe rubbed the soap bar between her hands, the scent of rosemary tickling her nose, then she scrubbed, rinsed, and wiped her face on the towel Antonia handed her, appalled when she saw the thick black streaks across the white.

"*Ancora.*" Again. Antonia smiled.

"She's going to kill me for that towel."

"Use more soap this time. And no, she won't."

Finally, Antonia relented and Chloe looked up into the mirror. Her face gazed back at her, open, her eyes huge and blue, her hair barely restrained.

"Essential ingredients," Antonia observed, "only the best."

"But *you* are beautiful," Chloe insisted.

Antonia laughed softly. "I used to say that to my mother all the time. She would be standing in the kitchen or digging in the garden, and I would think she was the most beautiful person I had ever seen. I was not a pretty teenager. And do you know what she would say to me?"

Chloe shook her head.

"She would say, '*Life* is beautiful. Some people just remind you of that more than others.' "

WHEN ANTONIA AND CHLOE got back to the kitchen, they saw Lillian had pulled a tray of chocolate éclairs out of the walk-in refrigerator.

"Stacy's specialty. There are a few left over from Sunday. Care to join me?"

"Really?" Antonia and Chloe eagerly settled in around the counter. Chloe picked up one of the éclairs and set it on a white plate that Antonia handed to her. She ran a finger along the top and felt the thick, heavy chocolate as it melted from her finger in her mouth.

"Uhmmmm. Tell Stacy these are wonderful."

"I like the filling best," Antonia remarked, delicately breaking the éclair in half and dipping the tip of one finger into the cream in the center. "My mother always scolded me for eating the inside of my pastries first."

Antonia's cell phone buzzed, and Antonia looked at the screen.

"How is it you say? Speak of the angel?" She saw their puzzled faces. "My mother," she explained. "Excuse me for a moment."

She opened her phone as she walked into the dining room. Chloe heard her voice as the door closed. "*Pronto? . . . Sì, ciao. Sto bene, e tu?*"

Chloe watched the swinging door for a moment after it had closed. She could still hear Antonia's voice, chattering delightedly.

"My mother and I would never talk like that," Chloe said, her voice like coffee left too long in a pot. She looked over at Lillian. "What about you?"

"We did for a while. She died when I was seventeen."

Chloe's face flushed red. "I'm sorry." Then, because she was young and incapable of not asking, "What did you do?"

"I cooked." The motion of Lillian's hands encompassed the kitchen and the dining room beyond. "And I was lucky—I had Abuelita in my life." She put her hand on Chloe's shoulder for a moment, then picked up the tray and carried it into the walk-in as Antonia came back through the swinging door, laughing.

"My mother, she likes to call me at this time," she said to Chloe. "She says it is the only thing that is good about my living so far away—she can wish me good morning and good night at the same time. Morning for her, night for me. And always, she wants to know when I am coming home to marry Angelo."

"Wait," Chloe interjected. "Who is Angelo?" Lillian, exiting the walk-in, raised one eyebrow.

"Oh, he is fine. A nice man. But he does not want to marry me and I do not want to marry him."

Lillian and Chloe looked at each other.

"I know who you want." Chloe's voice was mischievous. "But will he ever get up the nerve to do anything?" Antonia blushed.

"Now, Chloe." Lillian's admonishment was diluted by a smile she couldn't quite control. "We all know some bread just takes more time to rise."

Chloe laughed. "Yeah, well, I think it might be time to punch the dough, then."

. . .

CHLOE ARRIVED HOME at almost midnight that night. Jake was waiting in the kitchen.

"I thought you worked Monday nights?" Chloe asked.

"Not this late." He looked at her closely. "You look different. Where were you?"

"With friends." She read his expression. "I'm taking a class, okay?"

"What, getting ready for college?" Sarcasm curled up like a cat in his voice.

"A cooking class."

Jake's face closed so fast Chloe could hear the snap in the air. "I'm the cook," he said.

Chloe leaned against the doorframe, feeling the line of its wood along her spine. In her hand, she carried the tomato Lillian had given her, its weight solid and comforting.

"I think I might be, too."

"There's only one chef in a kitchen, Chloe."

Chloe pondered his statement for a moment.

"You know," she said, "I've been thinking that, too." She put the tomato carefully on the counter, then moved past Jake into the bedroom and started putting her clothes into brown paper bags. Jake didn't move. When she reached the front door again, bags in hand, she turned to him, nodding toward the kitchen counter.

"That's a good tomato—you don't need to mix it with anything."

She walked out, shut the apartment door behind her, and leaned against the jamb.

"Oh shit," she said, and giggled. "What am I going to do now?"

Isabelle

Isabelle entered through the kitchen door of Lillian's restaurant and halted, puzzled. There was so much activity, so
much food already sprawled across the counters. Was she late
for class? But even if so, who was the young lady spinning
between the stove and the sink where Isabelle always washed
her hands before the lesson started? Who was the man going
into the dining room with plates lined up his arm like pearls
on a necklace?

Isabelle stood in confusion. This was not the first time such
a thing had happened, as if life had suddenly put a different
reel in the movie projector midway through a screening. People
and images floating toward her, around her, leaving her hoping for a recognizable moment, a familiar voice or face upon
which she could anchor the rest and thus herself. At times like

these, Isabelle reverted to lessons from childhood. Her mother had always said if you are lost, just stand still until someone finds you.

"Isabelle." Lillian was coming up to her. Then it was all right, after all; if the cooking teacher was there, it must be time for the lesson.

"Isabelle," said Lillian, and her voice was sun on the grass. "Now, isn't that lucky. I wanted you to try our new menu, and here you are." Lillian's fingers touched Isabelle's shoulder, her smile wide and delighted. "I have the perfect table for you; we can sneak through the kitchen, like food spies."

Lillian gently took Isabelle's elbow and threaded her through the flying cooks and waiters, the celery tops and egg shells and tubs of clams and mussels, the smells of peppers in a hot pan and dishwasher steam, to the door that led to the din-ing room and sweet, soft candlelight, the clink of silverware against china, and the hush of heavy napkins dropping into waiting laps.

"Will this do?" asked Lillian, as Isabelle sank gratefully into a thickly upholstered chair. The table was small and round, set in an alcove looking over the garden. Isabelle could see there were people in the dining room; she wondered if the class was having a party.

"Is it Monday?" asked Isabelle.

"No, darling, Sunday. But you'll stay all the same, won't you? It would make me happy."

.   .   .

ISABELLE HAD ALWAYS thought of her mind as a garden, a magical place to play as a child, when the grown-ups were having conversations and she was expected to listen politely— and even, although she hated to admit this, later with Edward, her husband, when listening to the particularities of his carpet salesmanship wore her thin. Every year the garden grew larger, the paths longer and more complicated. Meadows of memories.

Of course, her mental garden hadn't always been well tended. There were the years when the children were young, fast-moving periods when life flew by without time for the roots of deep reflection, and yet she knew memories were created whether one pondered them or not. She had always considered that one of the luxuries of growing older would be the chance to wander through the garden that had grown while she wasn't looking. She would sit on a bench and let her mind take every path, tend every moment she hadn't paid attention to, appreciate the juxtaposition of one memory against another.

But now that she was older and had time, she found more often than not that she was lost—words, names, her children's phone numbers arriving and departing from her mind like trains without a schedule. The other day she had spent five minutes trying to put the key in her car door, only to realize that the automobile in front of her was simply similar to one she had owned fifteen years previously. She wouldn't have ever figured it out if the owner of the car hadn't come out of the grocery store and helped her, pushing that fancy little button on Isabelle's key fob, turning on the lights of her car three spots south, which was silver, not green, small, not a station wagon.

LILLIAN APPROACHED Isabelle's table and poured a sparkling dry white wine in a tall fluted glass. The pale golden liquid gleamed in the candlelight, mysterious and playful.

"Bubbles for your senses," Lillian said. "Enjoy."

Isabelle looked around her. The room was filled mostly with couples, leaning toward each other across tables, enclosed in their own spheres of candlelit intimacy. Fingers reaching toward fingers, or flying through the air, drawing the shape of a story. It made Isabelle wonder if rhythms could hold stories within them, if movements could jog memories the way a smell or sight could. Perhaps there were pathways in the air, created by her hands over years of relating anecdotes, waiting to take her back to stories she no longer remembered. She started moving her hands experimentally, then stopped. That was what old people did. She reached for her glass and looked nonchalantly through the window to the darkened garden outside.

. . .

SHE HADN'T EXPECTED the wine bubbles to reach her nose the way they did, like small, giggling children. Her children, two toddler girls, blond hair darkened almost to brown with water, in a bathtub only half full but still overflowing as they splashed, drenching her shirt and her stomach that held the third baby, their big, round laughter bouncing off the tile, letting out the day and leaving room for dreams. Edward arriving home, following the noise to the bathroom door, where he stood, adult and bemused, as she pushed the wet hair from her face and looked up at him. The girls later, dancing out of their towels and running through the living room, ripe-peach bums and big, proud bellies, until, finally imprisoned in pajamas, they settled on the couch, warm and sweet as new milk, while she read the story of the country bunny with the magic shoes until they quieted into sleep and she sat and thought about having golden slippers that would let her fly around the world and do extraordinary things and be back by morning.

LILLIAN SET a plate of salad on Isabelle's table.

"This is new," she commented. "I wonder what you'll think."

Isabelle dutifully took up her fork, skewering the leaves

of lettuce, bright and darker green, frilly magenta, the red of dried cranberries, and the pale moons of almonds and pears. The taste was the first day of spring, with the sharp bite of the cranberries quickly following the firm crunch of nuts, the soft-ness of pear flesh. Each taste here, defined, gone, mellowed only slightly by the touch of champagne vinegar in the dressing.

Edward. In the doorway, again, jacket off but tie still on, watching her make dinner in the kitchen. In her memories, it seemed Edward was always in a doorway, not quite there. As if she were the doorframe and the world were on either side. He wasn't leaving that time, although he would, later. When she was honest with herself, she would know he had always been on his way, either to or from her. Even after he left, he was on his way back, but by then she was gone, too, so light with-out the weight of his gaze upon her that she dreamed sometimes she was flying.

ISABELLE LOOKED DOWN—the empty salad plate was gone without her noticing, replaced by a dinner plate with a pool of white cannellini beans, atop of which sat a perfect piece of salmon, garnished with strips of crisp fried green leaves. Isa-belle picked up one of them experimentally and brought it to her nose. Dusty green, the smell of life made out of sun and little water, the driest of perfumes. Sage.

What she had wanted in the beginning was the desert, dry,

hot miles of air burned clean by the sun, the blank canvas of it after Edward and then the children were gone and she was left holding nothing and everything. She had gotten in the lumbering, wood-paneled station wagon and driven south, the fan whirring until she had turned off the highway and driven through cacti and hawks, opening the windows while the world flooded in, silver-green with the smell of sage.

At the town where she stopped to buy gas she saw a gallery, a spare, light-filled room with three white stone sculptures—smooth, white, sensual as dunes. While the gas station attendant filled the tank, she walked across the street and into the gallery. She looked at the sculptures, her eyes following the curves that made the stone seem more liquid than solid. Time slowed; there was no need to hurry—hers was the only car at the gas station. And as she studied each sculpture, she saw something else. It wasn't obvious—a line like an arm outstretched, a slope of a lower back, the hollow at the base of a neck where the collarbones meet—not a part of a person, rather the essence, the small vulnerable place where the soul lived.

"Stone poems," she said quietly to herself.

"Yes," said a voice, low and warm, and a hand touched her back, resting along the curve inside her shoulder blade.

His name was Isaac; he was younger than she, by years, his home far out in the desert, a red dirt house with faded blue shutters that held out the sun in the middle of the day, when Isaac worked with his eyes closed, smoothing the contours he had chiseled during the morning. A fountain murmured in the courtyard, under a tree, and Isabelle spent her first week sitting under its great branches, reading the books of poetry Isaac lent to her from the collection that meandered through his house, covering every available surface. They met each evening for dinner, pork stews that had simmered all afternoon, beans and rice. They talked over their meal, their conversations ranging like birds over the land around them. Isabelle slept in the second bedroom and woke each morning to the muffled sound of metal sliding through stone in the studio.

"What are we?" Isabelle asked Isaac one night, curious. They sat in the courtyard, smoke from the fire ring rising up between them, the stars huge and uncountable.

"Why do you ask?" he responded. A real question.

She had no sense of urgency; she felt like the desert, unending, sitting there in the dark. Still, she had felt she should ask the question, make sure she wasn't somehow disappointing.

"I think," he said contemplatively into the dark, "we are each a chair and a ladder for the other." And somehow that made sense.

It was Isaac who cut her hair. She was sitting in the courtyard with her head covered in pink curlers. He came out, wiping stone dust off the legs of his jeans, and saw her. His laugh bounced off the branches of the tree.

"What?" she said. "I'm not using a hair dryer. You don't have one."

He went back into the house and came back with a pair of

scissors and a straight-backed chair. "Come here," he said, patting the seat.

She sat in front of him and felt the curlers leave her head, one pin at a time, the damp, shoulder-length curls cooling in the breeze. When all the curlers lay in a pile around her, he took her hair and lifted it, cutting quickly and decisively, the weight dropping to the floor with the hair. When he was done, he ruffled her curls back in with his fingers.

"Now," he said, "just sit there in the sun and let them dry."

Her face, when she looked in the mirror later, was tan and younger than she remembered, the cheekbones stronger framed by the softness of the curls. She couldn't imagine the woman with that face having a cocktail party, wearing a blue wool dress cinched in at the waist. Handing her husband's secretary a glass of sherry, wondering what those slim fingers had touched.

Isabelle walked into the studio. "Thank you," she said simply.

He looked up. "Now," he said, "I think it's time for you to pose for me."

It MADE SENSE to stand naked in the studio room, her back to the open wall where the sun came in and ran down the length of her spine, the soft, rounded flesh below, the backs of her knees. She, who had never even stood naked alone in her own bathroom, welcomed the warmth, felt it center between her legs, at the base of her neck. She watched Isaac's strong brown eyes as they moved slowly and with a deepening understand- ing over her body, the softened angles of her collarbones, the slope of her waist rounding into her hips, the after-baby softness of her stomach, watched his hands as they moved across the stone, over the hours carving a curve that spiraled endlessly out into the world. The sex, when it happened late in the after- noon, was something both wanted but neither needed, as long and slow as the sun moving outside the shutters of the cool, dark room.

When she left, a week later, he stood at the door, watching her put her things in the car. She looked up and saw him and they smiled, long and slow, at each other.

He walked up to her. "For you," he said, and handed her a smooth oval of white marble that slipped into the hollow of her hand.

SALMON, THICK, DENSE against her teeth, a beach of smooth white beans underneath. Isabelle at six years old, throwing thin, flat rocks sideways, watching them sink and disappear while her father's floated across the surface, dipping then spinning up, like birds looking for food. The air cold and full of moisture on her face, even on a July morning, early, early, her mother and brothers still asleep, with just her and her father on the beach where she had found him, looking down the bay as if he could see what she couldn't at the other end. She had wanted to hold his hand, but her father wasn't like that, so she had picked up a rock and tried to throw it the way she had seen him do with her brothers.

"You'll kill the fish that way," he had said, as her rock plunged into the water like a lead ball, but his laugh wasn't rough.

"Show me?" she had asked, in a burst of bravery. And they had stayed on the beach while he showed her how to position the rock in her hand and snap her wrist and she threw rock after rock, until one of hers finally skipped, dancing on the water like a child.

"Time for breakfast?" her father had said then, and they had turned and walked back up to the cabin that waited where the rock beach met the big green trees behind.

It was only later, after her father was dead and she had children herself, that Isabelle realized that parents most often know when their children are stalling to hold off the end of something they want to hold on to. When she realized that there are many kinds of love and not all of them are obvious, that some wait, like presents in the back of a closet, until you are able to open them.

.   .   .

IT WAS THE CABIN Isabelle headed to after she left the desert. It wasn't a straight line—she stopped in Los Angeles and sold the family home; she spent time with each of her children as she moved her way north. The girls didn't understand. Grown now, one with a baby, the other in graduate school, they contemplated her from the cool remove of their new, adult selves.

"Mom, this is crazy. No one's been to the cabin in years. It's probably a wreck. And what are you going to do there all by yourself?"

They stood facing her like twin pillars of sensibility. Isabelle thought that if Isaac were to make a sculpture of them right now, it would hold the shape of an admonishing finger.

"Mom? What are you thinking?" Her daughters were looking at her expectantly.

"I'm thinking then you'll have to come and visit me." Knowing they would not.

Isabelle reached her son's house later the next day, as dinnertime was approaching. Rory lived in a big house in Berkeley, full of college roommates, who cooked together and laughingly muscled a capacious living room chair into the dining room so she could have a place at the table. She sat, distinctly lower in height, as they placed generous servings on her plate, insisting on mothering her, because, they all teased, she looked like a girl herself, with that short hair and tan skin, like she had been out climbing trees and needed a good dinner to fatten her up. Isabelle sat back in her deep, cushioned chair and listened to their good-natured voices, feeling both distinctly at home and ready to move on to her own.

Isabelle told her son her plan after dinner, sitting in the same chair, now back in its proper place. Her son considered her for a long time, and then smiled.

"I've got summer break coming up," he noted, "you might need help with that roof."

THE CABIN WAS worse than even she had thought. Windows broken, the roof barely protecting the squirrels that had set up lodging inside. The first thing she did, after spending a good week cleaning, was to build a shed for tools, but also for the squirrels, who eagerly vacated their former abode for one a little more private. The lines of the shed were hardly straight; Isabelle spent a lot of time asking questions at the local hardware store and trying to remember the lessons she had overheard her father teaching her brothers. But in the end, it had four walls, a roof, and a door that shut, with a shove, and the squirrels didn't seem like picky tenants in any case.

The cabin was nothing like the solid, square-cornered house she had shared with Edward and her children, but she discovered that was just fine, too. She cooked stews on the ancient white-enameled stove and baked brilliantly yellow cornbread in the oven. She found old glass, the kind that made the world outside appear as if it were underwater, and she fixed the bro-ken windows. She went to the not-quite-antique stores that pep-pered the side of the road leading to the national park nearby, and found an old bed quilt, blue and white, with stitches made by a hand she didn't know but trusted all the same, and laid it across the black metal bedstead. She discovered she liked the heft of an axe in her hand, the satisfying thud as it sunk into the log in front of her, the glistening white of the exposed wood as she stacked it on the pile.

On the night she got the phone line installed she called Rory down in California. She told him of her progress, made plans for his visit the next month.

"I think the roof will hold out until then." She laughed.

"Where did you learn to do these things?" Rory sounded amused. "I don't remember you fixing any windows at our house."

"You also don't remember that I didn't know how to cook when I married your father, or drive a car, or get a colicky baby to sleep. People learn, Rory. I'd hate to think there is an age when we have to stop."

On evenings when the air was warm, Isabelle would put on one of her father's old jazz records, open the door to the cabin, and walk down to the rocky beach. As the sun slid behind the top of the mountains, the sad, sensual sound of a trumpet, the low, deep voice of a woman in love, flowed out of the cabin like light from windows, and she would sit on a drift log, her toes playing among the stones, while the seals came up to the surface of the water and listened, their eyes dark and intelligent above the water line.

RORY CAME, as he had promised, when the days grew longer, clear and warm, stretching into evenings of abalone-blue sky. He was full of philosophy, his favorite class of the previous term, reciting passages of Plato and Kant as if they had just been written and he the first to find them.

Isabelle listened, watching the muscles move in her son's biceps and back as he ripped shingles from the roof and threw them down to her, wondering where the soft, round arms of her baby boy had gone, marveling at the beauty of her son standing above her.

"Philosophy and roofing skills," she called up to him. "You'll make some girl very happy."

"There is one," he told her, a little embarrassed. And then he had sat down on the edge of the roof and talked for an hour while Isabelle craned up at him and never once mentioned the crick in her neck because it was too precious to listen to her boy telling her with such beautiful naiveté about being in love, when all he had known was parents who hadn't been by the time he was born.

. . .

"MOM?" Rory asked one evening, as they sat on the beach watching the seals. Concert time, Isabelle called it.

"Yes?"

"Would you ever try marijuana?"

Isabelle laughed. "So this is what your college tuition is for?"

"Seriously, Mom. I mean, look at you. You're sure not the woman who married Dad. Have you thought about trying something really different?"

"I don't like to smoke."

"Well, we could work around that."

THE BUTTER SIZZLED in the pan, the leaves emitting a soft, smoky scent, not unlike sage, Isabelle thought. As she watched, the leaves softened, releasing their oil into the butter, while on the other burner, a brick of chocolate melted into a molten, glis-tening liquid.

"It's softer this way," Rory explained, "and you don't have to smoke."

They added sugar and eggs, flour. "Your father always liked brownies," Isabelle commented with a small smile as they put the pan in the big white oven.

They sat on the front steps, the smell keeping them company, thickening, deep and dense with chocolate. When the brownies were done, they ate them, still hungry from their day's work, even after a dinner of chili and cornbread.

"What are you thinking, Mom?" asked Rory after a time, wiping melted chocolate from his upper lip.

But Isabelle was flying, a mother bunny in golden slippers, looking down at her children, her husband, her house. Her cabin of her own, its roof almost finished.

"Isabelle," said a voice at her side. Isabelle looked up. She was in a restaurant. Lillian's restaurant. Of course. It was not cooking-class night—that had been silly of her—but then why was this young man, the sad one from the cooking class, standing by her table with Lillian?

"Isabelle," Lillian said gently. "I'm sorry to interrupt your dinner. Tom happened by, and the tables are a bit crowded. I hoped you wouldn't mind if he shared yours with you."

"Of course not," Isabelle answered automatically, motioning to the seat across from her. Tom sat and Lillian left them to check on a nearby table.

Isabelle shook off her thoughts and looked down at the last few cannellini beans left on her plate. "I'm afraid I am almost finished."

"Actually, I was hoping for just dessert and coffee. You can be my cover—that way Lillian won't get mad because I'm not eating a whole dinner."

"I haven't been someone's cover in a while," Isabelle answered with a laugh. She looked at the tables around them, many of which had emptied over the course of the evening, so that now the restaurant was only half full.

"Do you think she's expecting a late-night rush?" Isabelle asked, one eyebrow raised.

"I've been wondering," Isabelle commented reflectively over dessert, "if it is foolish to make new memories when you know you are going to lose them."

"And yet here you are, taking a cooking class," Tom noted.

"Well, not tonight, apparently," Isabelle pointed out wryly. Tom smiled.

They ate in an easy silence, reveling in the creamy lemon tart in front of them. After a while, Isabelle spoke again. "You know," she said, holding up a forkful, "I am starting to think that maybe memories are like this dessert. I eat it, and it becomes a part of me, whether I remember it later or not."

"I knew someone who used to say something like that," Tom said.

"Is that why you are sad?" Isabelle asked, and then saw his expression. "I'm sorry. My manners are going along with my memories."

Tom shook his head softly. "Your manners are fine—and

your mind is plenty sharp." He blew across the surface of his coffee, took a sip. "My wife. She died a little over a year ago. She was a chef, and she always used to say the same thing about food. I try to believe it, but it was easier when she was here and the food was hers."

"Ah"—Isabelle looked at Tom thoughtfully—"so we are not so different."

"How is that?"

"We both have a past we can't keep hold of."

"I suppose that's true." Tom looked at her, as if waiting for something more.

"I used to know a sculptor," Isabelle said, nodding. "He always said that if you looked hard enough, you could see where each person carried his soul in his body. It sounds crazy, but when you saw his sculptures, it made sense. I think the same is true with those we love," she explained. "Our bod-ies carry our memories of them, in our muscles, in our skin, in our bones. My children are right here." She pointed to the inside curve of her elbow. "Where I held them when they were babies. Even if there comes a time when I don't know who they are anymore, I believe I will feel them here.

"Where do you hold your wife?" she asked Tom.

Tom looked at Isabelle, his eyes full. He put his right hand to the side of his own face, then took it away and adjusted the shape slightly.

"That is her jawline," he said softly, running his left index finger along the half-circle at the base of his hand, then along the top curve where his hand met his fingers. "And here is her cheekbone."

TOM EXCUSED HIMSELF on the pretense of going to the restroom, and went toward Lillian, who stood by the front door, a wine-glass in her hand, receiving the compliments of a departing couple. Tom looked around the dining room and was surprised to realize it was empty, except for Isabelle at their table.

Tom walked up and touched her shoulder. "I'd like to pick up Isabelle's check," he said.

Lillian smiled. "It's on the house."

"Thank you for calling me. I don't know how you always know . . ."

"Lucky guess," Lillian said, raising her wineglass.

IT WAS COOL OUTSIDE, after the warmth of the restaurant. The streetlights shone through the new growth on the fruit trees of Lillian's garden. Tom walked with Isabelle along the lavender path to the gate; out on the street, people walked by, their voices animated by the prospect of spring, discussing bedding plants and summer vacation plans.

"Can I give you a ride home?" Tom asked.

"Lillian knows to call me a taxi," Isabelle said, motioning toward the street, where a yellow cab was pulling up to the curb. "My doctor says I'm not allowed to drive anymore."

"It was a lovely evening," Tom said. "Thank you."

Isabelle leaned up and kissed him softly on the cheek.

"It *was* lovely. Thank you, Rory," she said. She moved away and walked toward the cab that stood waiting under the streetlight.

Helen

Helen and Carl walked up the main street of town to the cooking class. It was a clear, cold evening in early February, the end of a miraculously blue day blown in from the north like a celebration. People in the Northwest tended to greet such weather with a child's sense of joy; strangers exchanged grins, houses were suddenly cleaner, and neighbors could be found in their yards in shirtsleeves, regardless of the temperature, indulging a sudden desire to dig in rich, dark dirt.

In the soft circle of lamplight ahead of them, Helen and Carl saw a man reach the gate of Lillian's restaurant; at the same time a woman approached from the other direction. The man unlatched the gate and stood aside to let the woman enter, his hand following her, unbidden, never quite touching her back and yet seemingly incapable of returning to his own side.

Helen watched the two walk up the path between the blue-gray lavender bushes—and the hand, the movement, the longing behind it, struck her with the intensity of a perfume she had long ago stopped wearing, drifting across a room she never intended to traverse.

HELEN HAD BEEN forty-one the first time she saw the man who became her lover. It was at the grocery store, a setting both absurd and logical for a woman who considered herself unequivocally married, who shied away from admiring glances at New Year's parties or darkened symphony halls or the weddings of dear friends where emotions, everyone knew, rode on high-speed elevators to greater heights than could ever be maintained the following day.

She had come to the store for eggs (Laurie had a teenager's addiction to egg-white facials), dog food, paper for Mark's new school notebook, steak for dinner (Carl's doctor said his iron count was low), and the usual—homogenized milk, Yuban coffee, Cheerios, rice, potatoes, paper napkins. She knew these aisles as well as her own kitchen, which was convenient, as a second list was running through her head—Mark to football practice, Laurie to piano, walk the dog, iron the tablecloth—a series of to-dos that moved in and out of her consciousness like breathing.

He was in the produce aisle. She wondered later whether anything would have happened if she had encountered him first among the cardboard boxes in the cereal section, spied him through the frosted glass of an opened door in the freezer department. But set amid the fecundity of late-summer melons and gauzy lettuce, swollen red peppers and plump navel oranges, he seemed simply beautiful in comparison, and any desire on her part more aesthetic than passionate. She watched his long fingers wander across the vegetables, reaching toward an onion, some carrots, opting for a bouquet of leeks. His eyes, when he looked up and saw her watching him, were infinitely brown and kind and his hair flowed in ill-kempt waves that he needed to cut but she immediately hoped he wouldn't, an almost maternal feeling—a rationalization that allowed her to step closer to the ocean that would surely soak her shoes.

He held up the vegetables in his hand. "My mother was French," he said to her, as if by way of explanation. "She was always asking me, 'What do you do that makes you happy?' Today, for me, leeks."

Helen stood, saying nothing, her hands empty. His eyes searched hers, and then he leaned forward, more serious, his voice gentle. "What about you?"

And Helen, who had begun to feel as if her life was like the daily turning of pages filled with other people's writing, felt as if she suddenly had come upon an illustration.

. . .

CARL CAUGHT the closing gate and pulled it open again for Helen. "Wasn't that Ian and Antonia?" he asked.

Helen shook her head, loosening her thoughts. "Yes," she replied, "I do believe it was."

"That would be nice for both of them, if that could work out."

"Don't be getting ideas about being helpful, Carl." The familiar rhythm of their banter was a bridge leading her back to him. "You saw how well that worked with our daughter." She touched his arm as she passed through the gate.

"But Mark is happy, and he gave you grandchildren." Carl's voice rippled with mischief.

They walked up to the restaurant, the garden around them February-quiet, all roots and no flowers. The bricks of the pathway clinked together under their feet in the cold; their breath moved ahead of them as if in a hurry to get inside the warm restaurant.

"I like winter," Helen commented.

Carl took her hand and drew her closer. "Good thing," he replied.

SHE HAD INTENDED to leave her marriage, was ready to tell Carl, her heart full of fireworks for this new man, the one whose clothes by the bed she had never bought or washed or mended, whose fingers slipped across her skin like a river, tracing cool, lingering trails to the inner curve of her ear, the slope of her hip, as if he was on a trip with no itinerary, no return date.

She had begun the conversation with Carl straight enough, readying the words she would use to help him accept the end of a union that had lasted longer than either of their childhoods. She had chosen the kitchen table, a place of domestic warmth, without the passion of a bedroom; they had planned vacations there, chosen health insurance, decided what to do with the dead guinea pig they found one Saturday morning before the children were awake. They had always worked well at this table.

Carl sat across from her. She saw his face, his eyes scanning her expression for hints of delight or anger or confusion, a road sign for the direction of their conversation.

He doesn't know what I am going to tell him, she thought. He doesn't know—and the idea struck her, strange as a bell mis-chiming. I know something about me that he doesn't. She couldn't remember the last time that was true. She looked at him watching her and she realized—not that it made any sense, but even so—that for her somehow Carl had always been with her, in her mind, in her body, in some unconscious but completely tangible way, through all the kisses and moans and explorations of her affair, just as he was when she gardened in the yard or cut her toenails sitting alone on the edge of the bathtub. After almost twenty years she simply carried him, a part of her, like blood or bones or dreams. But he hadn't been there. This man across from her, with his sandy brown hair and clear blue eyes, whose hands had held hers in childbirth and on every plane trip they had ever taken, was separate from her. And in that moment, Helen knew exactly what the pain of her leaving would look like, how it would wash across his face and turn his eyes a gray that would never exactly leave.

I would kill anyone who did that to him, she thought, and realized how completely that was true and that she could never do it herself. I love him, she thought, and the idea was as solid as the table between them.

Carl sat, waiting for her to speak.

"There was a man," she told him. "It's over now."

NOT THAT IT WAS; the body takes its time to follow where the mind leads. She never returned to her lover, but there were moments when she caught sight of a profile so like his at a traf-fic light that her body stopped, electrified, as if it was stepping without her consent into another life, as if being in both of those lives at one time, she might cease to exist completely.

If Carl knew it was not completely finished, it was not because she told him. He had entered the gray world of hurt, if not the one she had sworn to avoid, at least so close to it as to be easily confused. The irony of the situation caught at her, infiltrating her memories of her former lover until Carl became more a part of her lost affair than the man she had slept with. When she saw the men she thought were her lover, it was while driving her daughter to a sleepover, or carrying Carl's shirts from the dry cleaners, the smell of starch creating its own world around her. If she thought about the affair, it was while lying next to Carl, at night when everything in the house was finally quiet, with Carl's smell in the sheets, his breath playing across the pillow next to her. When she cooked using ingredients her former lover had introduced her to, standing half clothed in his tiny apartment kitchen, it was for her family, and over time the dishes acquired new meanings—Laurie's favorite dessert, the soup that made Mark eat vegetables, the stew that could be counted on to comfort for the loss of a football game, a boyfriend, a job offer.

So when she finally did see the man who had once been her lover—at her son's high school graduation, her daughter laughing and pointing at her brother, who was crossing the podium with just the slightest hop to his step—it was with the kind of longing we experience for something we never really intended to have in the first place. An older sister's boyfriend. A year in Provence. When her mind cleared, her son was across the stage, arms raised in jubilation, and Carl's hand was holding hers.

That night, after the cake and jokes and the symbolic glass of wine for Mark that everyone acknowledged was not legal but also not likely a virginal experience, after the children, who could no longer really be called children, had gone off to bed or parties, Carl had handed her an envelope full of the magazine pictures she had been cutting out for years.

"Provence," said Carl, and smiled. "A month at the end of August, when Mark goes off to college."

LILLIAN CALLED the class to their seats. "It's February," she began. "Almost Valentine's Day. I think Valentine's Day is a gift, like the weather we had today. Here we are in the midst of winter. Our skin has been hibernating in layers of clothes for months; we are accustomed to gray. We can start to think that this is how it always will be. And then, there's Valentine's Day. A day to look in your lover's eyes and see color. To eat something that plays with your taste buds and to remember romance.

"But here's the thing." Lillian ran her fingertips thoughtfully along the smooth surface of the wooden prep table in front of her. "If you live in your senses, slowly, with attention, if you use your eyes and your fingertips and your taste buds, then romance is something you'll never need a greeting card to make you remember."

Lillian looked out at her class, at Claire's hair, still tousled from her baby's exuberant good-bye, Antonia's sleek black work blazer, Tom's business shirt, rumpled at the end of a long day.

"It's not always easy to slow our lives down. But just in

case we need a little help, we have a natural opportunity, three times a day, to relearn the lesson."

"Food?" Ian suggested with a grin.

"What a lovely idea," Lillian responded.

"As a sensualist, your ingredients are your first priority," Lillian remarked, holding up the bottle of thick green olive oil. "Beautiful, luscious ingredients will color the atmosphere of a meal and whatever follows it, as will those which are mean and cheap." She poured a small portion of olive oil onto a plate, then dipped the tip of her finger in the liquid and licked it off contemplatively.

"Try this," she said, passing the plate to Chloe, who sat at the end of the first row of chairs.

"It feels like a flower," Chloe commented, sucking her finger to get the last of the liquid before passing the plate on to Antonia.

Lillian held up a second bottle, smaller and darker than the first. "Truly great balsamic vinegar is made through a long, careful process. The liquid is moved from one barrel to the next, each time taking on the flavors of a different type of wood— oak, cherry, and juniper—becoming denser and more complex with each step. Fifty-year-old vinegar is as highly prized and highly priced as great wine."

"Ian, hold out your hand," Lillian directed, and poured a few drops of balsamic vinegar, dense as molasses, in the curve of skin between his thumb and index finger.

"The best way to taste balsamic vinegar is with the warmth of your own skin," Antonia explained to Ian, holding out her own hand toward the bottle.

After everyone had tasted the liquid from both bottles, Lillian set them all to tasks, half the class grating cheese and measuring white wine and kirsch and cornstarch, the other half washing lettuce and cutting up tomatoes and baguettes.

"Helen, put the grated cheese and cornstarch in a plastic bag and shake it. The cornstarch will coat the cheese and it will melt more smoothly," Lillian suggested. "And, Carl, you can rub the inside of that red pot with a garlic clove. Some people like to leave the clove in the pot when they're done, or even add others to it."

"What are we making?" asked Claire.

"It's fondue, right?" Ian jumped in.

"Indeed. It seemed like a fun choice for Valentine's Day. Do any of you know where the word 'fondue' comes from?" Lillian asked the class.

"*Fondre*," replied Helen without effort. "It's French."

"To melt," added Lillian.

HELEN HAD ALWAYS wanted to live in France, although her French, studied assiduously in her early schooling, had over the

years of college and marriage and children become an attic collection, r's rolling like lumpy tricycle wheels, verb conjugations
jumbled together without labels or organization. She had bought
French audiotapes and the playful sparkle of syntax and syllables brought her delight, no matter how clumsy her attempts at
imitation. She had always wondered whether, if she was given the
chance, given a week, or two, to sink into another culture, this language would somehow rise out of her and become a way of thinking. What would she dream about, if she dreamed in French?

PROVENCE, when she and Carl arrived at the end of August,
had smelled of lavender—the air, the sheets, the wine, even
the milk in her coffee in the morning—the lightest of undercurrents, a watercolor world of soft purple. She found herself
breathing deeply and slowly, to pull it in, to hold it in every
part of her for later.

In the mornings they woke to songbirds and church bells,
then walked across the crunch of small white rocks in the courtyard of their bed and breakfast to one of the round green metal
tables set under a linden tree. They poured thick black coffee
from one silver pot and foaming hot milk from another into
wide white cups that warmed their hands as they drank. They
ate croissants that melted in their fingertips, scattering crumbs
that disappeared among the rocks, only to be found by the songbirds after they had left.

They rented a small car and spent days exploring roads that wound like grapevines up through towns set on the tops of hills, their limestone houses drenched in wisteria, their shutters pale blues or violet or faded sage green, the smells of lunch and din- ner slipping out of the windows like children, playing in nar- row streets that curved and meandered and made no sense, if only you cared about where you were going, which they didn't.

In tiny restaurants tucked into the corners of ancient, white towns, Helen and Carl made a pact, pulling out their diction- ary, Carl vowing to try any dish they couldn't find a translation for. To match his bravery, Helen shopped in the mornings at the tiny stores in their town and made fledging conversations with the fruit man until one day she triumphantly brought home a perfectly ripe melon, which they fed each other for lunch, its flesh warm and thick as the air.

It was hot in the afternoons, a heat that slammed through their open car windows and made them pant, pushed down on their shoulders and heads until finally they retreated to the shuttered cool of their room, to the delight of pounding water in their white-tiled shower, and finally to bed, where they stayed like teenagers until dinner. Only to do it the next day, and the next.

"This is why the Mediterraneans are so healthy," Carl had remarked one night, as he stretched his long arms luxuriantly above his head.

"*Oui*," she said, and smiled at him over a dish they had

thought would be a warm casserole but was, in fact, a cool assemblage of pink and white meats. (Should they buy a larger dictionary? they pondered. No, in fact, they would not.)

And that night she dreamed in French.

THE CLASS STOOD around the large prep table, two cheerful red pots perched on stands at each end, heated by small flickering silver cans underneath. The smell of warming cheese and wine, mellowed with the heat, rose languorously toward their faces, and they all found themselves leaning forward, hypnotized by the smell and the soft bubbling below them. Lillian took a long, two-pronged fork and skewered a piece of baguette from the bowl nearby, dipping it in the simmering fondue and pulling it away, trailing a bridal veil of cheese, which she deftly wrapped around her fork in a swirling motion.

She chewed her prize thoughtfully and took a sip of white wine. "Perfect," she declared.

Helen prepared a bite and placed the fork inside her mouth, the sharpness of the Gruyère and Emmenthaler mingling with the slight bite of the dry white wine and melting together into something softer, gentler, meeting up with the steady hand of bread supporting the whole confection. Hiding, almost hidden, so she had to take a second bite to be sure, was the playful kiss of cherry kirsch and a whisper of nutmeg.

"When you live with your senses, your gestures don't need to be extravagant to be romantic. I had a student once who courted a woman with fondue made over a can of Sterno in the middle of a park," Lillian noted.

"How did that go?" asked Ian, curious.

"Rather well," Lillian noted casually, "he got the girl."

The class clustered companionably around the two red pots; they fed themselves, they fed one another, stabbing their forks into the squares of bread and then submerging them in the fondue, laughing when the bread threatened to break free and their efforts at containment were not as graceful as Lillian's.

"*Sacrebleu!*" Carl exclaimed. "It is escaping!"

"Let me help you, good man," declared Isabelle, who only managed to push the bread from Carl's fork down into the molten depths.

"Aren't we supposed to kiss everyone when someone drops a bite?" Claire inquired.

"With food like this, who needs an excuse?" Carl responded, and took his wife in his arms to the admiring whistles of the rest of the class.

THEY WASHED their palates with white wine and sparkling water, and cleansed them with salads made from fresh lettuce, bursting red tomatoes, and thick, rich olive oil touched with balsamic vinegar.

"I feel completely alive," commented Claire. "I could run five miles."

"Perhaps that was not entirely the idea," Carl noted, smiling.

"And now," Lillian announced, "it is time for dessert." She displayed a long, slim chocolate bar. "The name for the cocoa tree is *theobroma*, which means 'food of the gods.' I know that chocolate is meant for us, however, because the melting point for good chocolate just happens to be the temperature within your very human mouth." She broke up the chocolate into bite-size pieces and put two on each small white plate.

"This is dark chocolate, which contains the most chocolate of all. No milk and not a lot of sugar added. At first you may think it is not sweet enough, but sweetness isn't everything. Let the chocolate dissolve on your tongue and see what happens."

She started handing the small white plates to each member of the class.

"Lillian, Helen doesn't eat chocolate." Carl spoke in a low voice as she reached him. "She gave it up years ago."

Lillian gave Helen a considering glance. "People change," she commented mildly.

Helen met Lillian's eyes, and took the plate she was offering.

THE CHOCOLATE ENTERED Helen's mouth, and the taste was there, as she remembered it—as if it was some deeper, richer

part of herself, all that was mysterious and yearning and passionate and sad somehow come together, washed up on the
shore of her imagination. And there in her mind, as she knew
he would be, in the place where she had hidden the memory
apart from the rest of her life, was her lover, his eyes dark, his
hands smooth as the sea, bringing her hot chocolate in bed on a
cold afternoon. An image held aside like a child's last piece of
Halloween candy, encapsulated, whether to protect it from her
marriage or her marriage from it, she could never have said.

Sitting in the restaurant kitchen, she heard as much as felt
the intake of her breath, then she stilled, holding her lover in
her mind, a perfect balance between pleasure and sorrow, as
the bite she had taken dissolved in her mouth and the memory,
released, flowed into her and became not the beginning or end
of anything, but a part of who she was and had always been.

She let out her breath and brought the chocolate to her
mouth again, inhaling its soft, dusty-sweet smell, like an attic
hung with dried lavender. And this time, what she saw was
the wide, white bed in Provence, the cool stiffness of the
starched sheets against their bodies still wet from the shower,
as she rolled on top of Carl and his eyes grew wide at her unexpected daring, then dark with pleasure as she moved gently,
then insistently, and his hands slid up her legs to grasp her hips.
The hours after, while Carl's tongue found its way across the
drops of water, then the sweat on her skin, as if she was both
completely new and utterly known to him.

And then another memory, as effortlessly as one wave following another—years later, Carl in her arms, his body pounded by sobs, her lips on his hair, whispering into its hot, damp depths that his father had loved him so much, that she was sorry, so sorry, that she was there would always be there, while he sobbed as if crying was a new kind of breathing and always would be until finally he slowed and she had held him, quiet, through the end of the day, while the noises of the road and houses and dinnertimes around them rose and fell.

And another—coming home one day to find a blank canvas and a box of oil paints—blue and violet and sage-green and white, terra-cotta and umber and brown—laid out on the small desk he had made for her that fit in the niche at the top of the stairs. Looking out the window above the desk she had seen an easel, set in the garden, spare and strong in front of the overgrown tangle of green and pink and white and yellow of their flowerbeds. She remembered the feel of the paint moving through the tube to the palette that first time, the brush meeting the canvas like a hand touching silk, Carl's pride when she had shown him her first painting, her own face lit with joy.

And finally—the sound of two pairs of pajama-clad feet coming to their bed early on a Christmas morning. Too small and, of course, too early. Carl's low, deep voice welcoming the toddlers into the warm circle of their two bodies, her arms reaching to enclose the sweet smell of her grandchildren, her hand touching Carl's face. And after, her thoughts too large for sleep, as she lay and watched them while Christmas morning came in through the windows.

"*C'est fini?*" Lillian was touching her shoulder gently, a stack of used plates in her hand.

Helen raised her eyes to meet Lillian's.

"*Oui,*" she replied, her voice soft. "*Merci.*"

And passed her plate to Lillian.

CLASS WAS OVER—the chocolate long gone, several more wine bottles emptied. Claire and Isabelle were on dish-duty, elbow-deep in warm water, washing the fondue pots and talking about tricks for helping a baby sleep through the night. Tom was helping Chloe with the recycling. After they finished wiping down the counters, Helen and Carl bid the rest of the class farewell and walked down the brick pathway from the restaurant toward the gate.

Ian stood in the kitchen door, watching them. In the mixed light, it looked at first as if Carl and Helen were following each other, but then Ian saw that their hands were linked, the edges of their coats brushing against the lavender bushes that lined the path.

"They are lovely together, yes?" Antonia came up next to him.

"They are." Ian paused. "I was wondering. I mean, I'd like to cook you dinner. Lillian is always saying we should practice and. . . ."

"Yes, Ian," Antonia replied. "I think I would like that."

Ian

"L illian's." The voice that answered the restaurant kitchen phone was young and masculine. The sound of dishes and voices clattered in the background. "How can I help you?"

"Is Lillian there? Tell her it's Ian."

The phone clunked down on the stainless-steel counter and Ian listened to the voices of the cooks in the background, their conversations slipping in between the sounds of chopping knives and water running over dishes and vegetables. Lillian's voice came on the line.

"Ian? What is it?"

"She said yes to dinner—what do I do now?"

"You cook, Ian."

"I know, but what?"

"Well . . . how do you feel about her?"

"She's beautiful and smart and . . ."

"I mean," Lillian's voice was patient, "what do you want?"

"I want . . ." Ian paused, and then his voice cleared. "I would want her for the rest of my life."

"Then that is how you cook."

THE GIFT CERTIFICATE for Lillian's cooking class—a thick, elegant, chocolate-colored card—had come in a birthday letter from Ian's mother the previous July. Ian had called his sister after opening the envelope.

"Do you know what she gave me? Cooking classes. Is there enough irony for you there? Cooking classes from a woman who almost never cooked—and when she did she burned what she was making because she'd get all wrapped up in some painting she was working on."

"Ian, I love you." In the background, Ian could hear the sound of toddlers claiming victory or possession, it was hard to tell. "It's your birthday. Why don't you give yourself a present and let go of some of that? She was an artist."

"But why cooking, of all things?"

"I don't know—maybe you should ask her." Ian's sister paused, and he could hear her taking the object of contention from one toddler, sending both howling companionably into the other room. "Are you going to go? To the classes?"

"Of course"—Ian's voice sounded defiant, even to himself—
"someone has to learn how to cook in this family."

WHEN IAN WAS YOUNG, he would sneak up to the attic space
his mother used as a painting studio. After the darkness of the
steep, narrow stairs, the light in the room glowed like sunshine
through flower petals, luminous and golden. His mother would
be standing with her profile lit by the window, brush poised in
one hand, surveying the canvas in front of her with an apprais-
ing eye. Still hidden by the partly closed door, he would wait,
not breathing, for the moment he knew would happen, when
her expression would clear and become joyous and the brush
would reach first for paint and then toward the easel.

During those early years, Ian associated the smell of paint,
thick and intoxicating, with that happiness on his mother's
face. The only time Ian had ever been scolded as a child—for
he was, in the main, a very good boy, never in the way, the
kind of boy who would always get the straight A's his parents cared little about—was the time when he had snuck up
to the attic while his mother and father were talking one evening and painted his hands so he could carry the smell with
him, thinking it would bring him the elation he saw in his
mother. His father was a bit taken aback by his blue-handed
boy; his mother, after explaining about the need to be careful
with special paint, had set him up with his own easel in her

studio, where for years he had worked beside her—caught up in the swirls, the shapes, the oranges and greens and yellows and reds, the way the brush moved the paint across the thick white sheets of newsprint—until he realized that other people never saw on the paper what had been in his mind.

"It doesn't matter, darling," his mother would tell him. "That's not the point of art."

But for Ian, who worshiped at the altar of clarity as only a boy careering toward adolescence can, it was exactly, precisely, the point.

WHEN HE WAS TEN, Ian had discovered computers. There were no computers in his house back then; his mother was more amused than interested by the concept and his father used the one in his office at work. But a friend from school had one, and Ian was smitten from the moment his hands touched the keyboard. Here was a partner of unceasing consistency, whose rules were inviolate, if only you understood them. And Ian did.

He badgered his parents for months, until the next Christmas there was a present just the right size under the tree. Ian sat by the box from the time he spotted it at four o'clock on Christmas morning until the time his family finally opened their presents and he could take his prize from its Styrofoam packaging and bring it alive. From then on, the computer, or one of its various successors, held court in his room. Over the years, more computers entered the home, but they were mere functionaries in the life of his family—mail carriers, research assistants. Ian regarded his computer as the best of friends, one that would unselfishly step aside for a new model with a better memory, a quicker wit. In a house filled with the ambiguities of color, Ian's first computers offered a reassuring world of black and white.

IAN HAD BEEN DETERMINED not to walk into Lillian's cooking class unprepared, so he had spent the month of August in his apartment kitchen. As a software engineer, he reasoned that cooking, like any other process, could be approached as a series of steps to be mastered, fundamental skills that could be applied even, or perhaps especially, when one was confronted by the chaos of complicated recipes, sinks overflowing with pots and pans, shelves of red and silver-green spices, hiding in small, round glass jars like memory land mines.

He started with rice—pure, white, elemental, an expression of mathematical simplicity: 1 part rice + 2 parts water = 3 parts cooked rice. Nothing extra, nothing lost. Cooking it required only a heavy pot and discipline, both of which he had.

It was a disaster. First he had too much discipline, and the rice on the bottom of the pot scorched, sending a sad, brown smell throughout the apartment; then he had too little, and the rice was soggy, refusing to be roused no matter how much he fluffed and encouraged. He added salt and butter, which at least gave the mush a vague resemblance to popcorn in terms of flavor, but it still was not rice. Not the way he wanted it.

It was abundantly clear that he was going to need help.

IAN'S APARTMENT was above a Chinese restaurant that he frequented more often than he would have cared to have his mother know. The dining room was small, its walls painted a color that Ian guessed had once been red, the menus faded almost to the point of illegibility.

The first time Ian had ventured downstairs to the restaurant was two years earlier, after a long, hot summer day spent moving into his new apartment. He had been tired and hungry, and after being seated by an ancient waitress whose formidable expression made him look surreptitiously at his watch to make sure he wasn't past closing time, he had opted for the safe choice and ordered sweet and sour pork and rice. When the plate arrived, he looked down at a fragrant mix of chicken, ginger, and the brilliant green of barely cooked broccoli tips.

"This is not what I ordered," he told the waitress, as politely as he could, not yet sure how varied his eating options would be in his new neighborhood.

She raised one impressive gray eyebrow at him, and left.

It was nine p.m. and he was the only customer in the res-taurant; as the swinging door closed behind the bowlegged gait of his waitress, he found himself alone with the plate in front of him. Uncertain if she would ever return and distinctly unwilling to follow the woman into the kitchen, Ian picked up his chopsticks and took a bite. The chicken was soft, delicate, the broccoli crisp and distinctly alive, ginger seasoning the mix like the provocative flip of a short skirt. The ache in his muscles from hauling and carrying moving boxes, the general anxiety that always encompassed him when he was confronted with the new and unfamiliar, left him like the last train of the day, leaving him calm and refreshed. He ate slowly and thought-fully, disregarding any thought of a take-home container for the next day's lunch. As he finished, the old woman returned.

"Good?" she asked. He nodded gratefully.

Her hands gathered the dishes roughly together into a stack. "You come back again," she said.

He did, and never once got what he ordered. He considered acknowledging the situation and simply declaring himself at the mercy of the kitchen, but then again, he realized he already was—his order simply a line in a play already written, with-out which the rest would not be the same. And so, each time, he stated a request he knew would be ignored and laid his trust at the doors of the kitchen, out of which, as if in recognition of a test he had passed, came dishes of delicate complexity and scin-tillating tastes, rarely if ever to be found on the actual menu.

. . .

THE NIGHT of the soggy rice, Ian left his failed culinary experiment and went down the faded red stairs of his apartment
building to the restaurant below. The waitress pointed to his
usual table by the window.

"Do you know how to cook rice?" Ian blurted out as he
was sitting down.

The waitress stared at him.

"I mean, of course you do; I just wondered if you could tell
me how."

"Why? You eat rice here."

"I want to learn how."

The old woman noted the urgency in his voice; she looked
at him more closely, nodded. "You don't cook rice, you take
care of it," she stated. "I'll get your dinner now." She returned
to the kitchen without even the pretense of asking him for his
order.

BACK IN HIS APARTMENT, Ian held a large metal bowl with a
layer of rice lying like an ocean floor underneath several inches
of cool water. He dipped his hand into the liquid and swirled
his fingers in a clockwise motion. He felt the delicate grains
slipping between his fingers, watching pearlescent white clouds

of starch enter the water like the changing of weather in the sky.

When the water was so thick with starch he could barely see the rice, he placed a colander in the sink and poured the contents of the bowl through it, the rice running out with the water like thick oatmeal until the last of it finally fell into the colander with a thud. He put the rice back in the bowl, filled it with water, and repeated the process, again and again, until the water stayed clear and he could see each grain of rice in the bottom of the bowl.

He drained the rice one last time and put the pot on the stove. He looked at the rice in the colander, plumped from its immersion, thought for a moment, then poured a bit less than two cups of water into the pot and turned on the heat.

ONCE IAN had perfected rice, he turned to polenta, then to fish lightly grilled on the hibachi he balanced on the pint-size balcony outside his kitchen window. By the end of August, he had placed small pots of herbs out on the balcony as well, the smell of basil and oregano and chives greeting his nose when he opened the window in the morning. He discovered a farmers' market near the bus stop on his way home from work downtown. He bought a good, sharp knife at a culinary store and began experimenting, slicing vegetables straight and julienned, cutting meat

with and across the grain, taking scissors to his basil, then ripping it with his fingers, to see if it varied the taste.

He found a store that sold spices in bulk, buying just as
much as he needed, which allowed him the excuse to return
and wander through the store, smelling containers with names
he didn't recognize. One time, he took a packet of an especially
intriguing spice into the Chinese restaurant and showed it to
the waitress. She inhaled deeply; then, with a look of amusement, she took the packet back into the kitchen, returning a
few minutes later with a dish redolent in its fragrance. Over
time, it became a game of sorts. At first frustrating, the recipes
for the dishes became something he looked forward to figuring
out, a challenge keeping him company, entertaining him in the
middle of a traffic jam or while he waited on hold for a service
call. He found himself eating more slowly, each bite a chance to
understand a part of the puzzle, until finally the puzzle wasn't
pieces, simply the feel of a warm sauce sliding down his throat,
the crunch of a water chestnut against the edge of his teeth.

By the time the cooking class started, Ian had more questions
than answers. He found himself reading chemistry books after
the cake-baking class, trying to make pasta on his own after the
Thanksgiving dinner. Watching the other members of the class,
he found himself wondering where they had come from, what

it was they brought with them, as if they, too, were recipes he might come to understand. Where Claire's face, that first night, had gotten its mixture of excitement and distrust, what made Isabelle recall the things she remembered, or what had placed Tom inside such an untouchable circle of sorrow. And then there was Antonia, always Antonia, with her olive skin and dark hair, her voice carefully finding its way around the American sounds and syllables that seemed too flat and awkward for her sensuous mouth.

He had found Antonia's hesitancy with his language endearing, and his desire to protect her was strong until the day he had encountered her at the farmers' market. He had recognized her from some twenty feet away and walked over, hoping he could help her past some language barrier, his assistance a worthy introduction to some other conversation. But as he got closer, he could see her hands flying, as if released. She was laughing, her words unintelligible to him but completely comprehensible to the Italian produce man in the stall, their faces beaming at the joy of playing in the waterfall of their own language.

Ian stood behind Antonia, breathing in her happiness, until the produce man sent him a sharp look and said something rapidly to Antonia, who turned to him, her face still lit from her conversation.

"*Sì, sì,*" she responded. "*Lo conosco.*" I know him. "Hello, Ian."

And without a thought, Ian's soul stepped into the radiated warmth of her expression.

. . .

A FEW WEEKS LATER, Antonia had called and asked him to help her. There were floors, she said, that needed to go away. So her clients would understand how important it was to keep things that were good and true. Ian didn't mention the apparent irony of getting rid of something in order to keep it; he just agreed and thanked the fates that had sent him a construction job that last summer before college, years earlier.

They had spent a long Saturday, pulling up squares of linoleum, downing cup after tiny cup of the espresso that Antonia made on the big black stove and that he hardly needed to get his pulse running. Midday, they took a break, and Antonia got out the lunch she had brought for them—hard-crusted bread and prosciutto and fresh mozzarella, a bottle of red wine.

"This is how we make a picnic in Italy," she told him, beaming.

"No peanut butter and jelly?" he asked.

"What is that?"

Ian smiled. "So, why did you move here?" he asked, curious.

She pondered the question for a moment. "Well, Lucca—the place where I grew up—it was wonderful, like a warm bath. So beautiful and everyone so loving. All the time, I knew what to do. If someone invited me to dinner, I knew what to bring. I knew the hours for the market. I could tell you, right now, when to catch the next train to Pisa. There was nothing wrong.

I just wanted—how do you say? a cold shower?—to wake up my soul."

Ian tried to imagine being so sure of what to do that he would leave everything, go somewhere else, just to be uncertain. She spoke so confidently, as if a warm bath was something you could to turn on any faucet to find. Perhaps, he thought, for her it was. Listening to her, Ian realized that he had spent his life in search of exactly what she had stepped out of. He was going to tell her this, but he stopped. Her face was changing expressions like sun moving over water, and he realized that more than telling her what he thought, he wanted to hear what she would say, wanted to watch her hands move in the air like sparrows.

"I remember," she said, "getting off the plane in New York. All those big American voices banging into each other. I had never heard so many. I thought I knew English, but I couldn't understand—the words would fly by and sometimes one would hit me and I would try to hold on to it. But they were very, very fast." She shook her head ruefully. "I felt so stupid."

"You are not stupid," Ian said emphatically.

"No," she responded, her eyes clear. "I am not. But you see, in the end, I think it is good to not know things sometimes."

"Why?"

"It makes everything . . . a possibility, if you don't know the answer." She paused. "I am sounding brave. I am not—I was scared. And it makes you tired, not knowing things. When I got here, I drank half-and-half for three weeks. I thought, Americans are so rich, maybe their milk is, too." She laughed.

"How is it now?" Ian asked.

"Better. I buy milk now." She smiled. "I am joking. But it is better. Every year I am here, I see more things that are familiar. I know that Americans carve pumpkins for Halloween, or send each other Christmas cards, or cook those big turkeys . . ." Her nose crinkled.

"You know what is best?" Antonia asked. Ian shook his head. "The cooking class. All those people, they all want to see something in a different way, like I did, but we are together."

She stopped, embarrassed. "I talk too much."

"No," Ian replied. "It is wonderful." He looked at her for a long time. "You know, I have always felt exactly the opposite. No, really"—he laughed, seeing her face—"all I ever wanted was to be certain of things. I listen to you, and it reminds me of this puppy I saw in the park the other day. He just leapt out into the lake after this ball. He never wondered if the ball would float, or if there was a bottom to the lake, or if he would have enough energy to get back to the shore, or his master would even be there when he got back . . ." Ian slowed, flustered. "Not that I think you are like a dog."

"Certainly not," answered Antonia, amused. They continued pulling up the linoleum for a time; the fir floors were showing clearly now, the glowing oranges and yellows in the wood changing the room, making it feel warmer, more alive, a part of the world outside as well as in.

"You know, Ian," Antonia commented, "my father always said a person needs a reason to leave and a reason to go. But

I think sometimes the reason to go is so big, it fills you so much, that you don't even think of why you are leaving, you just do."

"And you just believe you'll make it back to shore?"

"With the ball." Antonia laughed.

AFTER THE LINOLEUM DATE, as Ian preferred to think of it, he had a hard time concentrating on anything other than Antonia. Even so, it had taken him months to get up the courage to ask her to dinner. In fact, if it hadn't been for Lillian, and a vigorous poke in the ribs from Chloe, Ian might never have worked up the courage to ask Antonia to dinner at all.

But Antonia had said yes, as if perhaps she had been waiting, as if perhaps she had found his own hesitancy endearing, which only made him more nervous as the evening approached.

IAN PICKED UP the phone and dialed his mother's number. When she answered, her voice had the excited quality that Ian knew meant she was in the middle of a new painting.

"I can call back," he said quickly.

"No, I saw it was you." His mother's voice was happy. Ian pictured a painting filled with yellows and blues.

"How are you?" she asked.

"Everything's fine. Work is fine." He paused. "I'm taking the cooking class."

"How's it going?"

"Why did you give me a cooking class?" The words jumped from his mouth, unbidden. "I mean, you never cooked."

"No, not so much." Ian could almost hear his mother smiling.

"Then why did you give it to me?"

"Well"—his mother paused, searching—"when I paint, it brings me joy. I wanted you to have that, too."

"I'm not a painter, Mom."

"Perhaps not, but you are a cook."

"How did you know that?"

"Maybe it was your expression when you would taste what I made." His mother's laugh rang across the phone lines. "Don't worry, you really did try to be polite about it.

"So," she continued, "what are you going to cook for her?"

"Who?"

"The woman."

"How do you know there's a woman?"

"Ian, I may be a visual woman, but I do have ears." There was that smile again. "Besides, your sister told me. What are you going to cook?"

"I'm not sure yet," Ian hesitated.

"But you have an idea . . ." his mother coaxed.

"Yes," replied Ian, and suddenly he knew. "I was thinking

beef bourguignon. Something rich and comforting. With a deep red wine to match it. She's like that. And maybe a tiramisù for dessert, all those layers of cake and whipped cream and rum and coffee. And espresso, no sugar, for contrast."

He stopped, embarrassed. He realized he sounded like some-one he knew, and then realized he was talking to her.

IAN'S APARTMENT was small, the distinction between dining and kitchen table a psychological rather than physical one, and in any case only large enough for two. But Ian had bought a round white linen tablecloth and borrowed heavy silver candle-sticks from his elderly neighbor downstairs who required only that Ian tell her every detail the next day, a payment Ian sincerely hoped he would be able to mortgage. He had debated for a long half hour at the florist shop over what he should buy until the exasperated store owner had simply opened the huge refrigerator full of roses and daisies and carnations and shoved him inside.

"Choose for yourself," she said, and he had seen them at the back, resting quietly on a shelf above the white plastic buckets of red carnations and yellow daisies. Dusty dark purple tulips, their edges touched with black. They had cost almost as much as the bottle of Côtes du Rhône resting in the bottom of his shopping bag, but he didn't care.

. . .

THE BEEF BOURGUIGNON was bubbling in the oven, the smells of meat and red wine, onions and bay leaf and thyme murmuring like travelers on a late-night train. The kitchen was damp from the heat of cooking; Ian opened the window above the sink and the scent of the basil and oregano plants on the windowsill awoke with the breeze. He stood in front of the window, the warm water and soap slipping between his fingers as he washed the pots and pans, setting them to drain in the wooden dish rack, feeling the cool air run over his damp skin. When the kitchen was clean, he pulled out miniature bottles of dark rum and Grand Marnier, then the ingredients he had found at the Italian store on the other side of town—thick white mascarpone, whipping cream, bars of bittersweet and milk and white chocolate, glossy black espresso beans, and a blue box of pale *savoiardi* cookies. He laid them carefully along the counter, adding a canister of sugar and four eggs, cool from the refrigerator.

Ian looked at the assembled group in front of him. "We're making this for her," he told the ingredients, "and I've never done this before, so a little help wouldn't hurt."

He started with a thing he knew. From the cabinet next to the sink he took a small stovetop espresso pot, bought the weekend after the linoleum date with Antonia. As with making rice, the espresso pot had started out as a source of frustration, but over the weeks as he had practiced, learning the tricks and desires of the small, simple machine, the preparation of his small cup of espresso had become a ritual part of his morning, as necessary as a shower, as familiar and calming as watering the pots on his windowsill. So it was with a sense of easy affection that he filled the base with water and then ground the espresso beans. When the sound in the grinder changed from the rattling of beans to the breathy whirring of the blades, he stopped the machine and carefully spooned the grounds into the center metal container of the espresso pot, using the base of his thumb to tamp down the soft brown mass, feeling the grounds give beneath his finger like fine, warm dirt, the texture comforting, familiar.

How hard it must have been for Antonia, Ian thought, to leap across the ocean and leave all the sounds and smells, the tastes and textures she had always known. More and more recently he realized how much these very things made up his life. If he had told anyone at work about the little burst of pleasure he felt each time he opened the coffee grinder and released the smell of the grounds into his little apartment, they would laugh at him, and yet, these days, he noticed things like that. How his sense of balance was strengthened by the sight of the red walls of the Chinese restaurant below him or by the conversations the students had around the wooden prep counter in Lillian's kitchen after the class was officially over but no one really wanted to leave.

He placed the pot on the stove and listened again, as the water heated then boiled, rising like a little, contained tornado through the grounds until the coffee gurgled into the upper chamber and the kitchen filled with the smell, riding on the steam, pure and strong, like the first shovelful of dirt after a spring rain.

More than anyone he knew, Antonia carried these things with her, in the million sweet and careful rituals that still made up her life, no matter what country she was in. He saw it in the way she cut bread, or drank wine, in the whimsical tower she had made out of the ripped-up linoleum tiles, just for the joy of it, or perhaps for the expression on his face when he returned to the big old kitchen and saw it, a friendly welcome, a moment of creativity in the middle of a hot and dirty project. Antonia made celebrations of things he had always dismissed as moments to be rushed through on the way to something more important. Being around her, he found even everyday experiences were deeper, nuanced, satisfaction and awareness slipped in between the layers of life like love notes hidden in the pages of a textbook.

The espresso fell in a dark, silken stream into the small white bowl. Ian opened the bottles of rum and Grand Marnier, hearing the slight crack of the seal, breathing in before adding the soft brown and pale golden liquid to the espresso. The alcohol was strong and spicy; it seemed to glide effortlessly from the air into his bloodstream, from the bottle into the espresso, lingering there lazy and relaxed, two ounces of secrets waiting in the bottom of a bowl the size of his hand.

The large white eggshell cracked once against the side of the metal mixing bowl. Slowly, Ian slid the glistening orange yolk back and forth between the two cups of the shell, allowing the clear egg white to fall into the bowl below. The yolks he put in a small metal pot on the stove, spooning in sugar afterward.

And then he entered unfamiliar territory. The recipe told him to heat and beat the egg yolks and sugar until they changed color and formed ribbons, something "partway to zabaglione"— a term Ian didn't know. Antonia would know, he was sure, but Ian wanted his tiramisù to be a surprise. He took a quick look at the clock and saw with alarm that Antonia was due in fifteen minutes. He turned the heat on low under the pot, and put his laptop on the counter, searching the Internet for "zabaglione." Before he could get past the impatient prompting of the search engine asking him if he wasn't actually looking for a word with another vowel or two, the egg yolks in the pot were already curdling into hard, scrambled globs that no amount of frantic whisking could save.

Ian started over. Washed out the pot, closed his laptop. This time he picked up the hand mixer and let the beaters skim lightly over the surface of the egg yolks while they heated, pulling the sugar into the liquid as it thickened, forming small waves along the edge of the pan. He watched as the mixture became denser and he held his breath in anticipation of another catastrophe, but then as he watched, the eggs and sugar miraculously became lighter in color, a comforting yellow, the concoction falling in long, sinuous ribbons when he turned off the mixer and gently raised the beaters from the pot.

While the egg yolks cooled, he directed the beaters at the

egg whites, setting the mixer on a high speed that sent small bubbles giggling to the side of the bowl, where a few became many until they were a white froth rising up and then laying down again in patterns and ridges, leaving an intricate design like the ribs of a leaf in the wake of the beaters.

Next, the mascarpone. Lighter than cream cheese and a bit sweeter, it slid into the cooled egg yolks and sugar, making cream from custard, the color of sweet, freshly churned butter. The heavier egg yolk and mascarpone yielded with a sigh into the egg-white foam; under his hand the mixture grew ever lighter until it seemed to lift itself and the spoon moved through it all without effort.

The whipping cream was last, becoming firmer under the influence of the beaters rather than softer, the peaks finally reaching up to meet the beaters even as he pulled them away in order to add a soft snow shower of grated white chocolate.

Satisfied, Ian set the bowl aside and reached for the *savoiardi* cookies. He had had ladyfingers as a child—spongy, soft, part of a whipped chocolate freezer dessert, the oval cookies lined up vertically along the outside like debutantes in a receiving line. But the *savoiardi* were firm, delightfully crisp—if these were ladies, Ian thought with amusement, they were demanding respect. Ian laid them out, one after another, in a row along the bottom of a glass bowl and dipped a brush into the espresso and rum and Grand Marnier. He ran the tip of the brush smoothly along the top of the cookies, each stroke a bit longer than the last, and watched as the liquid sank deeply into their surface, like rain into desert sand.

When the cookies were dense with liquid, Ian gently, carefully spooned a layer of the creamy egg-white–mascarpone across them. When they were covered, he took a sharp knife and ran it along the edge of the bar of bittersweet chocolate, hard and dense, falling in a dark, velvety dust across the creamy white surface, then the milk chocolate, curling off like wood shavings. Then he repeated the whole process again and again until the bowl was almost full, a tower of cake and cream and chocolate. Lincoln logs all grown up, Ian thought, then spread an almost impossibly soft layer of white chocolate and whipping cream across the top.

Ian slid his finger along the edge of the tiramisù, bringing it to his mouth. The texture was warm, creamy and soft, like lips parting beneath his own, the taste utterly lacking in precision, luxurious and urgent, mysterious and comforting. Ian stood in the kitchen, waiting for Antonia, every sense in his body awake and completely alive, and thought that if the stars were suddenly to fall in a great, glorious burst into his kitchen, he would hardly be surprised.

Epilogue

The front door of the restaurant stood open, light spilling across the front porch and into the garden. Outside the gate, the world hustled by, running to the bank before closing time, getting off the bus from work. Inside, the garden was hushed and quiet. The Adirondack chairs sat empty in the cool evening air of early April; the branches of the cherry trees hung heavy with pink and white blossoms, their petals drifting like a spring snow onto the yellow daffodils below.

In the dining room the table was set for ten. The students had been arriving, walking up the path, calling greetings to one another, naturally gravitating in the direction of the kitchen door at the back, only to redirect their steps with a laugh of pleasure toward the front of the restaurant, where the smell of fresh bread and citrus beckoned them inside.

"We certainly are fancy tonight," Carl said as he entered. He handed Lillian a bouquet of cream-colored roses, intermixed with lavender and rosemary. "These are for you."

"How beautiful," Lillian answered, her voice lit with surprise.

"Essential." Helen kissed her on the cheek.

"I'll just get water for these," Lillian said softly, and went to the kitchen for a pitcher to put them in.

Isabelle approached the couple, her eyes dancing, her hand on Chloe's shoulder. "Helen and Carl, I'd like to introduce you to my new housemate."

"I'm like the puppy who showed up at the front door." Chloe grinned.

"And got a whole lot more than she bargained for," Isabelle added, chuckling.

"That's perfect," Helen replied, nodding in satisfaction. "And Chloe, you look simply beautiful tonight." Chloe dipped her chin, a small smile on her face.

"I think you might not be the only one getting a new room-mate, Isabelle," Carl remarked, raising an eyebrow in the direction of Antonia and Ian, who were talking together by the bay window, their fingers intertwined.

"Well, it's about time," Chloe said, returning to form. "Now, where's Claire?"

"I'm here, I'm here—the babysitter was late." Claire arrived laughing, bringing with her a tall man with curling blond hair. "I wanted you all to meet my husband, James. He's heard so much about you; it seemed only right he should come, and Lillian said it was okay.

"James," Claire said, leading him to the door near the kitchen, "this is Lillian."

While Lillian reached out a hand to greet him, Chloe ran up and pulled Claire away.

"Claire, I need your help with the salad," she insisted.

Lillian turned to James. "You have a lovely wife."

"Thank you," James said. His eyes traveled around the room, taking in the wooden wainscoting, the long table, the garden outside the windows shimmering in the twilight. "Did she tell you we got engaged here?"

"Yes," Lillian replied, smiling. "It makes me happy to know that."

"It's made her happy to be here." James looked over at his wife, laughing in the kitchen with Chloe. "Thank you."

"All we did was cook." Lillian reached up to brush at the rice cereal clinging to James's shoulder. "You did the hard work."

Tom entered the front door and Isabelle turned to greet him. "Tom, my white knight," she said, walking up to him, her hand outstretched. "Would you care to escort me to dinner?"

"I THOUGHT for our last session we should celebrate spring," Lillian said, coming out of the kitchen with a large blue bowl in her hands. "The first green things coming up through soft earth. I've always thought the year begins in the spring rather than January, anyway. I like the idea of taking the first aspara-gus of the year, picked right that day, and putting it in a warm, creamy risotto. It celebrates both seasons and takes you from one to the next in just a few bites."

They passed the bowl around the table, using the large sil-ver spoon to serve generous helpings. The salad bowl came next, fresh Bibb lettuce and purple onions and orange slices, touched with oil and lemon and orange juice. Then a bread bas-ket, heaped high with slices of fragrant, warm bread.

"I am eating spring," Chloe mused, taking a bite of aspara-gus. "I can't believe I've never liked vegetables."

"Something tells me you wouldn't get away with that at Isabelle's house," commented Claire.

"Lillian," Antonia called down the table, "I wanted to tell you—I have two new students for your next session. They just got married."

"And I bet they just happen to have a beautiful new kitchen to cook in," Helen remarked. Antonia nodded, blushing.

"Here's to kitchens," Carl proclaimed.

"And here's to what comes out of them," Antonia added, raising her glass to Lillian.

THE DINNER PLATES were empty, the last bites taken with sighs of satisfaction. Chairs were pushed back, and the conversations around the table meandered like tributaries of a great green river. Lillian stood at one end of the table and raised her glass, clinking it gently with her knife.

"I have an announcement to make," she said. The table quieted. "I'm going to have a new apprentice in my kitchen. I hope you all will come often and taste her cooking." Lillian reached into the corner of the room behind her and pulled out a set of chef's whites, which she placed in front of Chloe, who looked up, pride spilling across her face, while the class applauded.

"Oh, the sweet dear," Isabelle murmured to Tom, "I think she is going to cry."

"Now then, who is ready for dessert?" Antonia asked. "Ian has made something really special."

THE LAST DISH was washed; the kitchen floor was shining. Claire and James, who had offered to help with the last of the cleaning up, had put their aprons in the laundry basket and were walking down the path, Claire leaning in sleepily toward her husband's shoulder. Lillian stood by the wooden prep counter. The kitchen smelled of water and soap, the air vibrating with companionship and an undercurrent of desire as subtle as saffron, dusty-sweet as tarragon.

It had been a good class, Lillian thought, and spring was already in the trees. A new class would start soon. Lillian always felt a bit of sadness at this point, expected it even. This time, however, Lillian felt more regret than usual. She had always loved being the teacher, the one who knew the spices that would wake up a memory, heal a heart. She enjoyed holding the knowledge in her mind like a secret, figuring out which student needed which gift. But this class was different. These students gave to each other, reaching out among themselves with such grace. She saw how connected their lives had become and would remain. Where did a teacher fit in the picture, she wondered, when there was no longer a class? Lillian touched the tips of the roses softly and put them on the deep window shelf.

The teacher fit in the kitchen, of course. Shaking her head at herself, Lillian walked to the back door.

"Lillian?"

Tom was standing at the bottom of the stairs, his collar pulled up against the cool of the evening air. In a garden full of cherry trees, she smelled apples.

"It's still early yet," Tom said, his voice reaching across the space toward her. "Would you like to take a walk? I have a story I'd like to tell you."

Lillian gazed back into the room behind her, its counters clean, the walk-in ready for the Tuesday deliveries. She listened to the quiet hum of the refrigerator for a moment, the whispers of the flowers in the vase. Then she turned off the light, and left the kitchen.

Acknowledgments

This book was a gift, given to me by many people. Marjorie Osterhout's generosity of time and spirit touched every page. Gloria Attoun asked perfect questions and created beautiful illustrations. Rebecca Sullivan proved, yet again, her skill and patience as a friend, reader, and photographer. Sydney and David Oliver gave me Paris in December. The Blue Ribbon Cooking School, Julie Logue-Riordan, Jeff McLean and Dian Campbell, Lisa Cooke and Mark Rechtin, Val and Simon Griffith, were sources of delightful culinary inspiration. Mark Craemer, Nina Meierding, Michael Bauermeister, Deedee Rechtin, Peggy Sturdivant, and Holly Smith read with open hearts and clear minds. MJ Rose opened doors for someone she barely knew. Josh Getzler was my fierce advocate; Amy Berkower, an extraordinary agent; and Rachel Kahan, an insightful and ever supportive editor. And always there are Caitlin, Rylan, and Ben—I love you.

ABOUT THE AUTHOR

Erica Bauermeister received a B.A. from Occidental College and a Ph.D. in literature from the University of Washington. She is the coauthor of *500 Great Books by Women: A Reader's Guide* and *Let's Hear It for the Girls: 375 Great Books for Readers 2–14.* She lives in Seattle with her husband and their two children.